Trampled Shoots

by

P F Cairns

Astwood Publishing

© P F Cairns 2013

Published by Astwood Publishing Ltd
Astwood House Carnoustie Angus
DD7 6LW

Website: www.astwood.org.uk

ISBN 978-0-9566732-7-5

Cover design by Sanctus Media
Tel: 01506 827217
Website: www.sanctusmedia.com

Disclaimer
The characters of this novel are all fictitious, and any possible likeness to anyone living or dead is purely accidental; each character has been developed from the author's imagination. Similarly, the village communities are entirely fictitious.

Acknowledgements

My grateful thanks go to:

My husband, Alan, and our family for their love and support.

My many friends who have read the manuscript and encouraged me to publish 'Trampled Shoots'.

My Soroptimist friends who have opened my eyes to the suffering of women and girls around the world. Soroptimist International raises issues such as: domestic violence, trafficking, the forced marriage of young girls and the reluctance of some countries to educate girls. Soroptimists work both nationally and internationally to educate, empower and enable women and girls. Please see http://www.soroptimistinternational.org for more information.

To Neil MacLennan and Rae Manger at Sanctus Media for preparing the cover and creating the book's website: www.trampledshoots.org

Preface

Katie Baxter was disappointed that she couldn't join her brother, Tim, on a return trip to the Amazon jungle. Twelve years earlier, then only children, the siblings survived a horrific plane crash over the Peruvian jungle. After three months in the tropical forest, and with the help of some Amazonian tribespeople, the youngsters were eventually rescued.

Tim, a naïve young man, is a junior doctor who has just finished his initial hospital training. His Amazonian friend, Miguel, asks Tim to come and work in his jungle village for a few months. The clinic in Intuto, the regional town high up on the River Tigre, was usually staffed by a government doctor but he had returned to the city of Iquitos and there would be no replacement for many weeks. Tim just couldn't refuse the challenge. In the village, the medic's clinical knowledge is quickly put to the test. But nothing prepares him for the night he awakes to the pain of a pistol pressed hard against his temple.

Back in the UK, Katie is studying journalism at university and has a work placement, over the summer holidays, with a daily newspaper. Her initial few weeks are boring and mundane until she is given a seemingly simple assignment. The trainee interviews Judith and her teenage daughter

Laura; the story they tell, shocks the student and sends her researching the murky world of organised crime.

A fast paced novel, based over two continents, where two young adults fight against the evil that confronts them … but both refuse to give in.

Contents

Chapter 1

Flashback

Late on an August afternoon the riverboat, Nimrod II, slipped her moorings and crept out of the Port de Iquitos to join the mighty Amazon River. As Tim Baxter watched the ship manoeuvre into the giant waterway, he couldn't believe it had been twelve years since he had stood on this same deck. This was the vessel that had brought him, then a young teenager, and his young sister Katie from deep in the rainforest back to civilisation. An amazing coincidence, he thought.

As he stood looking upstream he remembered how these had been desperate times for him and his sister. Their nightmare had begun as they flew home to Scotland to visit their grandparents. His family had relocated to Lima when his father, Alex, took up his post as an executive with an oil company. Neither parent could take holidays during the school vacation so Tim and Katie set off on the trip home in the company of their aunt. But shortly into the flight the aircraft was downed by a severe thunderstorm. Miraculously Tim and Katie had survived. The two endured the hardships of the jungle for three months and would have remained lost, possibly for ever, had it not been for the help of three native brothers, Miguel, Ronaldo and Pablo.

Tim shuddered as he recalled how the brothers had rescued Katie and him just as the two of them were about to stumble across a terrorist group; realising their worth these fighters would have surely kidnapped the gringo youngsters. These were the same bandits who had terrorised Miguel's community forcing the villagers to flee to a remote settlement deep in the jungle. It was in this isolated village that Tim and Katie were looked after by the indigenous people.

He could picture the village, with the flimsy houses built on stilts, new ones being constructed, others repaired. He could hear the laughter of the children as they dived and swam in the river to cool themselves from the heat of the sun. He could see the hunters returning in the evening proud of the fresh meat they had killed with their blow darts; the smell of the cooking pots and roasting spits was so clear to him again as he was transported in his mind back to his jungle home. The tribe treated him and Katie so well; Tim knew they owed them their lives.

But there was one big problem: the chief had refused to let them leave in case the terrorist gang should find out where the community had escaped to. The criminals had killed three of the village elders at the outset and so the chief was not going to risk any others of the tribe.

Tim recalled how after a few weeks in the village, Katie had become very unwell with fever and the traditional remedies hadn't worked. Miguel, an intelligent young man, recognised that Katie was very ill; he was frightened she would die as his own young sister had done a few years before. Miguel had come across western medicine and he knew she could be treated. So against the wishes of the chief, he and his brothers helped Tim and Katie escape from the remote jungle village. Now an adult, Tim recognised this was a very brave thing to do. Within the Amazonian tribal system the village chief was never challenged!

The brothers decided to take the young gringos to a medical post on the Napo River and then once Katie had recovered, to catch the riverboat to the jungle city of Iquitos; there the Baxters would be able to contact their parents. Because they had disobeyed the chief, the three brothers could not return to their village so they took the big decision to travel to Iquitos with Tim and Katie and to start a new life there.

Many thoughts continued to flash through Tim's brain as he relived his first visit to the Port de Iquitos. Stepping off Nimrod II, all those years ago, should have been the end of their ordeal but within half a mile of the harbour a new, even more terrifying, turn of events began.

The group had no money and were all very scruffy and dirty, so it was impossible for them to make the quick phone call to the children's parents. They had been given the contact details of someone who would help them in the shanty town of Puerto Belen. The youngsters set out that very dark night along the street to the township; Tim and Katie planned to ask the police for help if they came across any officers on the way. They believed their luck had turned when, after a short distance, a police truck stopped a few metres in front of them and two big men in uniform jumped out. But the two naïve gringos soon realised they were in real danger when the officers drew their batons and started to run towards them.

Standing on the deck Tim could feel his whole body tense as he again pictured in his mind the ferocity with which the policemen attacked the group. Miguel was knocked unconscious; Pablo and Ronaldo tried to help him, all the time shouting to Tim and Katie to run! The brother and sister did take off but were pursued by the police.

Tim was having a flashback now. He was beginning to sweat and feel nauseous, his hands trembling; he had remembered the police dogs. He could hear the growling of the big Alsatians and could see them tear down the hill towards him and Katie; if it hadn't been for Rico.

The young man pulled himself together, releasing his grip on the riverboat railing; he hadn't had a full-blown flashback for several years now. They used to happen several times a week, waking him from sleep, his mother rushing through to his bedroom to calm him and assure him he was safe.

But where was Rico now? Tim wondered. Probably dead he thought; he knew that street kids had very little chance, dying from disease or violence. If only Rico had come back another night to Gilberto's soup kitchen. How much he and Katie owed to Gilberto. This selfless, kind man had been a former employee of the oil company that Tim's father had directed. A Christian man, Gilberto grieved for the street children of Iquitos; most nights of the week he could be found feeding the boys down by the Rango Bridge.

After their rescue the Baxter family founded a street children's charity in Iquitos and for almost ten years Gilberto had directed the work. Many abandoned boys in the city had been helped by the charity but Tim realised there was still much more to do. If only, Rico had been found, he wished.

A speedboat roared past the bow of Nimrod II and disturbed Tim's contemplation of past events. Trying to think of other things he started to look round the battered vessel. It was as run down and filthy as he remembered; the boat didn't even look as if it had been painted. As with the previous journey the vessel was jam-packed with people, but the cargo was quite different. There were no bananas or other fruits piled high on the deck heading for the city markets, but rather foodstuffs and provisions destined for the townships on the river. Palettes of Coke, Inca Kola and beers were a sure sign that the river communities were catching up with the western world. As it was holiday season for most westerners the riverboat had many travellers on board: Americans, Europeans and some Japanese. All sporting the best of jungle gear, mobile phones and expensive cameras.

Tim was a doctor now, a graduate of St Thomas's in London; he had just finished his first two years of hospital work. Although he wanted to be a paediatrician, a children's doctor, he didn't feel ready to start the eight year training programme. He decided instead to head off around the world, working as a locum, gaining valuable experience as he went. He and Katie had visited Iquitos many times over the years as they had kept close ties with Miguel and his brothers. Tim knew Katie was really disappointed not to be with him on this, his first trip back into the jungle.

Miguel was a teacher and worked in the regional town of Nauta; he had married Maria, a local girl, and together they had three children but recently their lives had changed. Miguel's uncle, Bruno, the chief of their home village, had sent a message to the teacher asking him to return to the jungle. Bruno was ill and knew he was dying; he had to appoint a successor and Miguel was, to him, the obvious choice which surprised the younger man. Miguel had always believed that he couldn't return to his village after defying his uncle. But Bruno had mellowed and was secretly very proud of his nephew's achievements. The Peruvian army had successfully brought the terrorist problem under control, so the old chief had felt it safe enough to leave the remote jungle and had established a new village high up on the River Tigre just west of Intuto.

Nueva Casa, as the village was known, was growing with many new families joining the community; they had a dilapidated school building but no teacher. So Miguel would be able to work professionally in the new village but he wasn't keen to move his family into the jungle so far away from Iquitos. His daughter, Jessy, was nine and would soon be old enough to go to secondary school; Miguel was determined she was going to have the chance to continue her education. He knew that in the villages the girls were expected to marry when they were still very young and so they could never gain a decent education. Miguel knew how important it was for all children to go to secondary school, but he felt he owed his uncle so much – the chief had taken in Miguel and his brothers when they were orphaned by the death of their father in an accident. The teacher agreed to help for a short time but was undecided about succeeding his uncle as chief.

So in February at the height of the rainy season, when the rivers were full to overflowing in places, Miguel and his family travelled, by riverboat, the one hundred and fifty miles upstream to Nueva Casa.

Tim had intended to go to Australia, New Zealand and finally to Peru on his way home the following year, but these plans all changed after an email he received from Ronaldo, Miguel's younger brother. Ronaldo lived in

Iquitos and worked as a carpenter; he loved computers and so kept in regular contact with Tim and Katie. Miguel sent a message to Ronaldo to ask Tim to come and help in the village for a few weeks. The doctor at the health post in Intuto had moved on to a promoted post but the replacement wasn't due to arrive for another two months. Bruno was very sick and Miguel was 'acting' as headman already. Many of the children were badly nourished and some had died. This would indeed be a challenge for the young doctor, one he couldn't refuse.

The journey to Nueva Casa would take three to four days stopping at every community on route. Tim wasn't particularly looking forward to being cooped up in the run down vessel. From his initial scan of the boat the sanitation was no better than before; a stinky area behind a polythene sheet! The kitchen area, which was just next door to the loo at the back of the vessel, showed no obvious improvements either. Where were 'Health and Safety Regulations' when you need them? he wondered.

Ronaldo had insisted on accompanying Tim on the trip which would be a great help to the young medic. He had a large backpack full of medication for the village so travelling with his Peruvian friend would make it so much easier to look after the precious cargo and deter any thieves. Tim's belongings comprising of mainly T-shirts and shorts were crammed into a small pocket on the rucksack; the rest was stuffed with antibiotics, rehydration salts, worm tablets and much more. As they headed upstream and away from civilisation, Tim was extremely thankful that he had spent his two month student elective period in a mission hospital in Papua New Guinea; at least he had some knowledge of tropical medicine!

The two friends had decided at the outset that they would take turns to sleep so they only brought one hammock. They tied this up on the middle deck, towards the bow, to get some shade and be well away from the odours of the stern. Tim offered to let Ronaldo sleep first, so after the first meal of chicken and rice Ronaldo headed for the hammock. Tim carried his backpack to the bow and took in the stunning view of the setting sun, way to the west. The brilliant yellow colours of the sun quickly changed to darker hues as the deep orange ball slipped beneath the horizon; suddenly Tim's world and that of his fellow travellers was plunged into darkness. The few lights that remained on board were buzzing to the sound of the thousands of mosquitoes that had flown from the riverbank to the beacons, bringing with them their potentially deadly bite. The locals were unperturbed: dressed in T-shirts and shorts, lying unprotected on the deck or in hammocks with no mosquito nets. Most of the tourists had enough sense to don long-sleeve shirts and trousers. Tim was annoyed with himself for not putting his trousers on sooner as he muddled about in the dark searching the pockets of his rucksack; he hoped that Ronaldo would have been a bit wiser and put the mosquito net up in the daylight!

The young doctor propped himself up against his backpack on the top deck well away from any lights. As he lay there looking up at the beautiful night sky, crowded with many more stars than he would ever see at home, he thought of what might lie ahead. He hoped he would have the skills for whatever came his way but he knew he was still very junior in his profession and there would be no senior medic to turn to. As his heart rate began to rise in his chest he calmed himself with the realisation that the community he was going to had no medical care at all so surely he could help in some way. He contented himself with the knowledge that God, who had rescued him from the jungle all those years ago, loved him and would be with him throughout the trip.

His thoughts were interrupted by a young American talking to his friend. They were discussing the distance to the Hatin reservation. Tim had heard of this place and knew something of its reputation for offering tourists a taste of the ancient practices. Tim shuddered when he realised these two young guys were about to risk the rituals of the village shaman; all in an attempt to find their true selves! Tim had been coming back and forth to Amazonia long enough to know that dabbling with such occult practices was not 'cool'.

Chapter 2

Summer Placement

Katie was so angry with herself! If she hadn't agreed to do another attachment she would have been going up the River Tigre with Tim. *The Newburgh Herald* didn't sound that exciting either but she knew she would reap the benefit after she graduated; the extra four weeks' experience with the daily newspaper would help her in her quest for a full-time job in journalism. These days every employer was looking for more than good qualifications; they were also demanding experience and lots of it. A good degree was essential as well, and Katie knew that her final year was going to be tough. But if she had known that Tim was going to Nueva Casa to help Miguel she would have taken her chances on the employment front and booked a flight with her brother.

Trips to Peru were almost an annual event for Katie. She, like her brother, loved nothing better than to arrive in Iquitos and meet up with Miguel, Ronaldo, Pablo and their families. The Baxters had kept very close contact with the Peruvian boys and developed a close brotherly friendship with them. Katie was very fond of Miguel's children. Ronaldo's wife, Carmen, was in the early stages of pregnancy with their second baby; sadly their first child had died of meningitis when only two months old. Pablo was a student and still single; he was desperate to be a translator for one of the many sightseeing companies working in and around Iquitos. He had an excellent command of English thanks to his friendship with the Baxters, but he was also very competent in German.

It would be September before Katie would be free to travel out to Peru. She could manage two weeks just before the start of her final year at Reading University but knew that there was no way she could go unaccompanied to Nueva Casa. Sadly it was unlikely she would see Miguel and his family this year. She knew that Tim would be back down river about then anyway. All in all she felt quite frustrated but then thought maybe there was a reason for it.

At the end of August, her parents were coming back to London for a two-week holiday so she would be able to spend time with them. At least her parents weren't boring or control freaks; they always had fun together. Katie's parents had been working in Kolkata for the past five years. Her father, Alex, was an executive with UNICEF in that great city, working with the local community to set up educational facilities for street children. Sarah, her mother, was a freelance investigative journalist with a special interest in the rights of women and girls and was currently working closely with members of the Dalit caste, the lowest group within Indian society. Katie always loved to hear about their work. Her ambition was to follow in her mother's footsteps and use her journalistic skills to help girls rise out of the slums. Katie had been to India on many trips, often staying for several months with her parents. She loved the country and was completely overawed by its vastness and complexities. It was a huge country, the seventh largest in the world, with a population of over one billion. Katie saw it is a country of contrasts: a rapidly expanding highly educated middle class yet millions denied access to decent education due to their lowly caste; a nuclear power yet millions living without clean water and sanitation; sophisticated cities surrounded by squalid slums.

———◦———

Monday morning, six o'clock sharp, the alarm on the Katie's mobile woke her from her slumbers. An eight thirty start was always going to be difficult for this Arts student whose norm was to work late and rise very late. But Katie had heard that the editor at *The Herald*, Sandra, was one of the old school, a middle-aged lady with a bite to match her bark and she expected her staff and especially her trainees in the office on time! Katie knew that it would take her half an hour to shower, dress and have breakfast and that the drive would take at least forty-five minutes. If all went well she should be in the office just after eight.

Arriving in plenty of time, the young trainee was shown to her work station by John, one of the reporters, who worked on the news desk. He had been charged by the editor to be Katie's mentor. John didn't look much older than Katie but she discovered that he had three years of experience with the paper since graduating and he was something of a favourite of Sandra's.

Katie's first encounter with the boss went much better than she could have hoped. Sandra, was dark-haired with a hint of grey at her temples and had a dress sense ten years out of date, but she seemed to be interested in Katie's training and she promised the student lots of opportunity to learn her craft if she applied herself.

John came over just as Katie was settling into her small space, in a corner of the office next to the water cooler.

'I've a job for you,' he smiled. 'It's just right for the trainee.'

'Oh good, I can't wait to get started. What is it?' Katie replied, enthusiastically.

'There's a new old folk's home, being officially opened this afternoon, at Craigsbank. Lady 'somebody' is cutting the ribbon, sometime. Your job is to find out some details: some background to the Lady, how many old dears there'll be on the granny farm, who's the farmer etc, etc?' John said, in all seriousness.

Katie was taken aback at John's disrespect for the elderly. She could only think of her own grandmother who would have been disgusted at being referred to as an 'old dear' or at any suggestion that she lived on a 'granny farm'. But Katie felt she didn't know John well enough to say anything.

But John realised he had shocked his young colleague by the look on her face.

'Sorry, who is the owner of the residential home for the elderly?' he smirked. 'Here's the address and telephone number. The manager will be pleased to hear from you; her boss will want as much publicity as possible. Bert the freelance photographer will be there too.'

Katie smiled as she accepted the scrap of paper with the contact details from John. She knew she had to get it right and not muck up on this her first assignment! The trainee noted down exactly the information she needed to make the article as interesting as possible. Next, Katie decided to phone the manager and see if she could meet with her before the opening ceremony, but first the young reporter decided it would be worth carrying out an internet search to see what Craigsbank Care Home was saying about itself to the world.

A few 'clicks' later and Katie found the home page of 'Tundergarth Care Homes'. She discovered that this was a fairly big organisation which ran about twenty residential and nursing homes in the Oxford area, but this was the first home in Newburgh. Katie was able to take a virtual tour through the new purpose built home. She was really impressed by the facilities: each resident had a spacious room with en-suite shower room; there was a sitting room with a large television; a sunny conservatory and a beautiful garden for the residents to stroll round.

Further down the page was a link to the opening ceremony where Katie found out who the dignitaries would be. Lady Helen Grimshaw was to be the guest of honour; some local councillors and social workers from the borough would also be attending. Once Katie had researched a little of the background of Lady Helen, she felt ready to telephone the manager and ask for an interview.

The manager of Craigsbank agreed to meet Katie at the care home for a chat, but at ten o'clock! Katie, a stranger to Newburgh, looked at the clock; it was nine thirty and she had no idea how to find Craigsbank. The reporter was quickly on to the Tundergarth Homes website again downloading the map. Three minutes later she bolted for the office door.

'You're in a hurry! Where are you off to?' John asked inquisitively.

'I've an appointment at ten. Can't stop or I'll be late.'

John smiled at the new recruit's enthusiasm. He was very glad that Katie had arrived at *The Herald* as he didn't have to cover such ridiculous events as opening ceremonies and fêtes; he would get some real journalism now, at least for the next month.

Ten minutes to ten and Katie was driving around in circles looking for Pitt Crescent; Craigsbank was first on the right up this street. There was no one around to ask so Katie became increasingly anxious that she was going to be late.

Finally she caught a glimpse of 'Pitt' and turned into the street but two hundred metres further along discovered it was a dead end!

A three point turn later and Katie and her little Mini car headed back down the road; a left turn at the end brought her safely into Pitt Crescent. Two minutes later she was running up the steps of Craigsbank Home but it was five minutes past ten! She couldn't believe it, she had blown it on her first assignment; she was late!

'You must be the reporter,' a voice said, coming from the bottom of the steps, behind Katie. 'I'm sorry I'm late, the traffic was awful this morning. I hope you haven't been waiting long.'

'No not at all. I'm Katie Baxter,' the reporter replied, extending her hand courteously to the older woman.

'Come in and sit down. I'm Jane Cuthbert, the manager here. Reporters are getting younger and younger, or maybe I'm just getting older. Now, what would you like to know? Would you like some coffee?'

Ms Cuthbert spent over half an hour with Katie, much to the student's surprise. The manager supplied Katie with more information about the home and the type of residents in her care. She discovered that Craigsbank was designed specifically to look after patients with dementia and that Lady Helen, as well as being a local dignitary, was a member of The House of Lords and Chair of the Alzheimer's Society.

Katie returned to the office after assuring the manager that she and a photographer would return in the afternoon to attend the opening.

Back at her desk Katie researched Alzheimer's disease to find more information and statistics about the illness. She wanted her article to be more than just about Lady Helen cutting a pink ribbon while wearing a navy blue hat! Katie was determined it would be an informative piece.

By the time Katie arrived home that night she had submitted her first article to the editor's desk. All she could do now was wait and see if her work would reach the standard expected.

———◆———

Day two in the newsroom of *The Herald* was very hectic for Katie. She was paired up with one of the more senior journalists, Alf, who was looking into rogue property factors.

Alf explained that reports had reached the paper of problems in some of the new blocks of flats. Owners were being charged high annual fees by companies who were supposed to look after the grounds, the lifts, the stairwells and the like, but often the work was not being done.

Initially Katie thought this would be interesting and her first taste of investigative journalism but in reality her job turned out to be a real bore. She had to sit at her computer and find out if these 'rip-off' factors had been uncovered in other cities around Britain. It soon became evident to Katie that Alf had been 'landed' with the trainee and had to find her something to do; he was off into the town to speak to the flat owners, the work she wanted to do.

After three hours of research, Katie had discovered considerable information about 'bad' factors, especially in Glasgow and London. But the tedium of the job was getting to her; as she stared out of the window at the lovely sunny day, Katie's thoughts turned to her brother. She wondered if Tim would have arrived at Nueva Casa or would he still be on the riverboat. Katie longed to be back in the jungle instead of stuck in front of a computer screen; she rued the day she had decided to take on the extra placement.

Her thoughts were interrupted by John, 'The editor wants to see you in her office, now.'

Katie gulped hard. 'Sandra hasn't liked my article – oops!' she muttered under her breath.

'Okay, cool! I'm on my way.'

The trainee knocked nervously on the editor's door.

'Come in. Katie, a good piece of writing; you have put in a lot of effort, but needlessly. Look, this is all we can print. These sorts of items are more about the photograph and only a little about the blurb.'

Katie walked behind Sandra's desk to look at her computer screen. Bert's shot of Lady Helen cutting the ribbon was at the top of the page with a 'two liner' comment underneath. The rest of the page was full of other community activities such as WRI, Rotary club reports and pictures of golfers receiving their trophies at interclub competitions. The student's heart sank; all that effort she thought.

'I know what you're thinking,' Sandra commented. 'All my effort, wasted.'

Katie smiled and nodded in agreement trying not to show how disappointed she was.

'To save yourself a lot of time, time that you'll not have when you're employed as a reporter, follow the instructions given to you by your editor. Yesterday you were asked to report on an opening ceremony not write a feature article on dementia!'

The trainee looked sheepishly at the floor as the editor continued, 'Have I made my point?'

'Yes. I'm sorry.'

'That's all,' the editor said as she flicked to the next screen.

The rest of the afternoon Katie was decidedly 'hacked off'; annoyed with herself for trying to be too clever with the article and frustrated that so little of it would be published. By the time she got home that night she really wished she had gone to the Amazon!

Chapter 3

River Trip

The noise of the riverboat as it manoeuvred into the jetty woke Tim from his dreams. It took him a moment or two to realise where he was. The gentle swaying of his hammock and the strong smell of diesel quickly reminded him that he was not in his London flat, nor was he about to dash to his hospital ward at St Thomas's for the morning ward round. Much to his relief his days as the house officer or general 'gofer' on the ward had finished ... well at least for now. No, he was heading for the jungle.

Nauta was a busy community on the banks of the Maranon, an upper tributary of the Amazon. The town lay just up river from the confluence of the Maranon and the Ucayali rivers; two thousand miles from the Atlantic Ocean. This was the township where Miguel and his family had set up home; it had a population of about ten thousand people, many of whom were very poor. Miguel had been one of the teachers in the primary school for almost eight years, a job he loved.

Tim scrambled out of his hammock and up to the top deck to find Ronaldo; he was dutifully standing beside the medical pack. The noise was even more intense now as the vessel chugged to and fro to settle the bow in just the right position. The dark blue smoke of the overworked engines filled the air so much that Ronaldo began to cough and splutter but it soon cleared when the engines were cut. The entire manoeuvre was watched by a crowd of fifty or so people standing on the jetty. Tim noticed how substantial the pier was here; a concrete construction, something he hadn't seen before as jetties were usually wooden and quite flimsy by European standards. This was different; there was even a corrugated roof to shelter passengers from tropical rains, a sure sign that there was a very vibrant tourist industry in the area.

There was a good tarmac road between the city of Iquitos and Nauta, the only tarred road out of the regional capital. The friends could have come the sixty miles by car but Tim had experienced the wild and reckless driving of the taxi drivers so many times on visits to Miguel, that when Ronaldo suggested the longer and cheaper journey by riverboat he had not protested. Tarmac surfaces were such a novelty to these drivers that when they were behind the wheel they thought they were competing in a Formula One race! Tim shuddered as he recalled the last journey he had made in one of the taxis: no seatbelts, bald tyres, overladen vehicle, going round corners on the wrong side, it was a wonder he had survived.

From the deck Tim and Ronaldo could see that many of those waiting on the quay were westerners. Some were clambering onto small launches and heading out into the river towards bigger craft, others were waiting patiently in line to join the riverboat.

'Where do you think they're off to?' Tim asked.

'By the look of that smart vessel over there I think they

are going to cruise up river, possibly to the nature reserve. They say the accommodation on these vessels is wonderful: air-conditioning, proper beds, and highly trained chefs but all very expensive. My friend's brother works in the galley of one of these ships; he says it is usually fully booked!'

'Looks like a bird watching trip; lots of expensive cameras and binoculars swinging around. I would love to go on one of these expeditions,' Tim said.

'Just think, these gringos will have paid lots and lots of dollars for the trip. When you get to Nueva Casa ask my cousin to take you into the jungle,' Ronaldo suggested. 'Pedro, he's very good; he knows just about every bird in the rainforest, probably more than the guides on the tourist trip!'

'Yes, I bet he does. When we lived with you in the jungle I don't think bird watching was of much interest to us. I do remember Miguel showing me lots of different types of birds though, but I've no idea what they were called,' Tim recalled. 'I'll ask Pedro to take me out on a trek; I'm sure he'll teach me a lot.'

'Hey Tim, there's the police launch pulling into the smaller jetty over there; away to the right of the pier. Do you see them?'

'Yeah! Look! They're "off loading" three men in handcuffs. I wonder what they've been up to. The officers aren't taking any chances: two with machine guns on the bank watching the prisoners disembark and two other officers behind them,' Tim noticed.

'Listen! Here comes the police truck,' Ronaldo replied. 'They must be big crooks!'

The two friends watched as not one, but two police pickups screamed along the front of the port area towards the jetty. The truck at the back had five or six heavily armed officers standing in the rear, the vehicle at the front was a locked van ready to take the prisoners.

'They must be drug traffickers,' suggested Ronald. 'There wouldn't be all this fuss for some petty thieves. The police are obviously terrified about a possible ambush. Look the policemen have their faces covered, a sure sign that it's to do with cocaine smuggling.'

'You're probably right. Miguel mentioned that there had been a number of high profile arrests in the drug world recently. He said things were much safer in the region: fewer shoot-outs and less kidnapping. Let's hope it stays that way.'

'It would be good if these terrorists were all locked up because that is what they do, they terrorise communities. Poor people just want to live quietly in their villages, they don't want to be threatened and coerced into growing coca plants or setting up cocaine factories,' Ronaldo commented, in sombre mood.

'Remember what happened to our village all those years ago,' he continued. 'The three elders, the brave ones, who refused to be intimidated or escape with the rest of the villagers into the jungle; they were killed. But hopefully things will be better in the future. Our government has spent a lot of money in recent years with many more soldiers stationed here now.'

'I hope you're right. The big problem is that in Europe and America organised gangs make a fortune selling cocaine. They're not going to give up without a fight. It might be quiet just now but as soon as the government in Lima cuts back, they'll return!' Tim cautioned.

'Let's hope you're wrong!'

'Hey, Ronaldo! There's one of those American medical boats; I wonder where he is going.'

'He's certainly not going up the Tigre. It's the dry season now so the rivers will be very low. That ship looks as if it has quite a deep keel, so it would definitely get stuck on a sandbank up there. She's probably heading back to Iquitos; I hope the captain's a local man as even on this stretch of river the vessel may have difficulties reaching the city without a close encounter with a sandbank,' Ronaldo remarked.

'Surely not on the main river Amazon? I thought it was really deep in this region.'

'There are sandbanks shifting all the time round here. That's why it needs to be a local registered captain or they must hire a pilot,' Ronaldo asserted.

The two friends passed the time watching the passengers and cargo load and unload from the riverboat; crew members working speedily to ensure a quick turnaround. Within an hour the ropes were untied and Nimrod II, the ramshackle boat with the grandiose name was continuing its journey upstream.

Tim just loved to find a spot on the deck right at the front of the ship; there he could sit and watch the world go by as the vessel trundled upstream against the strong current. His favourite perch was in front of a pile of flour sacks, in the centre of the bow. The medical pack acted as a barrier between him and the crates of hens that shared this area of the deck and he could enjoy the added bonus of a back support from the baker's stores.

On his previous voyage on the mighty river system, the young boy hadn't appreciated the power of the river, its determination to flow onwards to the ocean no matter what stood in its way. The marooned areas of land that were now small islands were testament to this. On his last trip Tim was a frightened teenager; the wonderful creation that was around him was inconsequential to a lad of his years and in his predicament. But now as Tim soaked up the beauty of the vista in front of him he marvelled at the amazing world in which he lived. The river beneath, he knew, was teaming with life and much of it undocumented by scientists; in parts of the massive river system the waters were so deep that even powerful search lights couldn't penetrate the darkness. The forests on either bank of the river were filled with creatures large and small: from beautiful parrots to tiniest winged insect each expertly designed. There lived large jaguars, small rodents, beautiful camouflaged frogs and many more fantastic creatures carving out different sorts of life cycles yet in a marvellous way interdependent on each other. The more Tim thought about the marvels of this tropical region the more he could see the hand of his Creator at work.

Tim's clear view of the river ahead was broken by a large vessel coming downstream. It looked huge as it came round the corner and for a while Tim couldn't work out what it was. Ronaldo arrived with a bottle of Inca Kola for his friend and saw the puzzled look on Tim's face.

'It's an oil barge. It's bringing crude oil from the wells just to the north of Barranca,' Ronaldo said with certainty. 'The locals say the oilmen are making a terrible mess; many hectares of forest have been destroyed already and they've only been working in the region for the past two years.'

'Have you been up there?'

'No, but I met some of the Mantou people in a bar in Belen. They were the local tribe in the Barranca region but they had to leave. The men folk were mainly hunters but the destruction of the rainforest has driven off all the animals. The rivers were poisoned too by the sludge from the well head. With no fish and no meat, the headman had to act. He tried to speak to government officials but they just ignored his pleas. They told him that it was in the interest of all Peruvians that the drilling went ahead. With no help from officials the chief decided that the villagers had to move on or they would starve. Some of the men folk had heard that life was good in Iquitos and so they brought their families downstream to the city, others moved away to other regions to set up a new community.

'I bet they've changed their mind about Iquitos. No doubt they're living in Belen. With no skills it's no surprise they've ended up in that awful slum,' Tim commented.

'Yes these guys and hundreds of others from all over Amazonia! In the past few years the central government has granted many oil exploration licences, all in the name of progress, but sadly with little thought of the impact on the local tribes folk,' Ronaldo griped.

'It has happened in many nations: the country dwellers are forced off their land by oilmen or miners. Sometimes the rural folk think life will be better in the cities so they pack up and move to the towns, but they can't find work and so end up in the squalid conditions of the slums. It's not just a feature of South American cities but Nairobi in Kenya, Lagos in Nigeria, Kolkata in India, in fact all over the world,' Tim expounded. 'The United Nations reckons that by the middle of the century a quarter of the world's population will live in slums.'

'What's the United Nations?'

By the time Tim had explained the machinations of the

great world organisation to Ronaldo it was almost noon and very hot; the friends moved to the portside to take advantage of the cool breeze that was blowing down river. As they rounded the next bend the riverboat headed north from the Maranon up the Rio Tigre. This Amazonian tributary drew its waters from the plains between the Maranon and the Ecuador border. Like most rivers in that part of Peru it was a communications lifeline for the villages dotted along its banks. Along the first mile or two from the confluence of the two mighty rivers there were many communities nestling on the banks, so the riverboat made very slow progress on its journey northwards.

'How long is this river, Ronaldo?' Tim asked his friend as they watched yet another fast boat speed past their lumbering vessel.

'Not sure but I think it gets pretty close to the border with Ecuador.'

'Intuto is quite far north isn't it?'

'Yeah, I just hope this old tub can get up there! The river level is way down,' Ronaldo warned.

'I see what you mean; the banks are about four to five metres high. No wonder they cut steps into the banking! I know it's the dry season but is the water level lower than usual at this time of year?' Tim asked, unsure of the normal variation in river level.

'Yes, the rainy season was unusually dry this year which has had this knock on effect. Of course the amount of rain that falls in the mountains impacts downstream,' Ronaldo explained. 'It would be rare not to get up as far as Intuto, so don't worry.'

'The locals are always inquisitive when a boat goes past, aren't they? Look there must be twenty kids waving from the bank,' Tim said as he returned their greeting. 'The children must take turns to act as "lookout" so that when something interesting comes along the word goes round like wildfire.'

'Yeah I guess so, but my people are very friendly,' Ronaldo said with a smile. 'I'm hungry; I'll go and see if I can get some bread.'

Tim continued to watch the world go by. He thought how lucky he was to be able to join Miguel and hopefully help out for the next few weeks. He shuddered a little at the thought of coming across some medical emergency or tropical disease that he didn't know how to handle. Thank goodness for the little 'Handbook of Tropical Diseases', that he had brought with him, and that he had managed to stay awake on the plane to read most of it! But what if there was a difficult birth, someone needing surgery to deliver the baby? Tim could feel his pulse quicken just thinking about it. He had assisted at many caesarean sections but had never actually carried one out himself; besides he had no intentions of being a surgeon. But now even his palms were sweaty; someone needing a section would be a nightmare scenario!

Chapter 4

Tropical Storm

The next twenty-four hours passed pleasantly for Tim. Most of the time he sat in his prime position at the front of the riverboat thinking things over and watching the most amazing scenery go by. Mostly the jungle came right down to the riverbank but in places, often on a bend in the river, there would be a clearing where a small community had been established. Tropical birds would dart in the high canopy or gracefully soar along the banks before swooping up to the trees. Tim never tired of watching the ever-changing vista.

The young doctor was glad of the rest. Only a few days before, he had finished a tough six months working in the general surgery unit in one of the busiest hospitals in London.

He wasn't short of sleep but was grateful for the 'down' time. Being one of the juniors on the surgical ward was full-on from the moment he stepped on the ward until he left at the end of his shift. Tim's boss Mr Brown had a reputation for being an ogre; this man had a way with words that could make even a tall six-footer like Tim feel about eighteen inches high. At first Tim found this very intimidating, but as the weeks went by he realised that if he worked hard and to the high standards that his consultant expected, their relationship would improve. Tim began to understand that Mr Brown demanded the best for his patients and therefore required the best from his surgical team. Unlike most surgeons that Tim had encountered, this man would take time to sit beside his patients and answer their questions; always trying to make them feel at ease and allay their fears. The young doctor soon stopped moaning about the early ward rounds. They might begin at least half an hour before those of the other consultants but the time was well spent.

Most of Tim's work was routine: admitting patients, organising tests, speaking to relatives, but if one of the trainee surgeons was on holiday or on study leave Tim would assist Mr Brown in theatre. These were long hard days of standing and holding retractors while the great man chopped, removed or joined up bits of bowel like an expert seamstress making an intricate wedding gown. Tim couldn't help but admire this surgeon, who was now close to retirement, his stamina was greater than a man half his age. In the changing rooms, before the surgeon went through to the theatre, he always bowed his head for a few moments. On one occasion, when there was only the two of them left in the changing rooms, the older man caught Tim watching him.

'You don't think I open these people up on my own do you, Tim? I always pray before I leave home in the morning and before I start my list. Does that surprise you?' the surgeon asked.

'No, I thought you might be a Christian. I've never heard you swear or blaspheme. I am too, ever since God rescued me and my sister from the Amazon,' Tim replied.

'We must invite you round for Sunday lunch. My wife would love to hear of your adventures in the jungle. But enough! It's time for us to scrub up and start work,' Mr Brown adjusted his surgical cap and pushed through the swing door into theatre with the young novice close on his heels.

Tim recalled how Mr Brown had encouraged him to take a year out before settling into his training job. The surgeon was of the firm belief that every young doctor should experience another nation's health care systems or help out in a developing country, before they embarked on the long grind of specialist training. Tim chuckled to himself wondering what his old boss would think of his current assignment.

'Why are you smiling?' Ronaldo asked breaking the silence.

'I was just thinking about my old boss ... wondering what he would think about me going to somewhere as remote as Intuto and being the only doc,' Tim replied.

'Yeah it's quite remote. But don't worry, you'll do a great job,' he said encouragingly, with little clue of the burden of responsibility about to be placed on his friend's shoulders.

'Hey look! There's a pink dolphin: no there are two, three ... lots of them,' Tim shouted excitedly as he grabbed his camera and jumped to his feet.

The two young men spent the next half hour or so just watching the antics of these strange creatures. Being so agile made them very difficult to photograph so Tim had to use the video option on his camera. He spotted the hump on the dolphins which was quite different to the dorsal fin on most fish; some of the creatures were two metres long and a grey-ish pink while others were much smaller and a deeper pink.

'These are magnificent creatures. I think I've managed to get a few on film. I'm surprised we haven't seen some before now,' Tim commented.

Ronaldo explained to Tim that the species was now under threat. In the past villagers treated them with respect as they believed that they had magical powers and so would never harm them, but others now saw them as competition: a threat to their own fishing so would catch and kill them. Dolphins also died after becoming entangled in fishing nets or being poisoned from the pollution that was steadily increasing in the river system.

Darkness fell suddenly as usual, but only after an amazing sunset. Tim had managed to capture a fantastic still shot; one he hoped would be good enough to print up when he returned home. Away to the north they could see fork lightning and by the increasing intensity of the thunder it was heading their way. The two men didn't have to wait long before a ferocious storm was right overhead. For Tim the noise of the thunder was almost overpowering, the boys had to retreat to under the top deck in an attempt to find shelter but by the time they reached cover they were soaked. The wind was roaring through the ship; lights initially flickered off and on, then darkness, complete darkness; the generator had 'packed in'. A few minutes later as Tim was searching through his rucksack for a torch the vessel's engines spluttered to a halt!

'We're in trouble now,' Ronaldo shouted in Tim's ear, against the noise of the wind and torrential rain. 'We'll drift downstream and quite quickly, if the captain doesn't get that engine started soon.'

'The river is so twisted on this stretch. I counted at least six really sharp bends just before sunset and many of these had large sandbanks well out into the river,' Tim replied, understanding the reason for Ronaldo's concern.

'Yeah! And these are the ones you can see. You'll have noticed that the captain has kept the vessel in the middle of the river ever since we turned north up the Rio Tigre … that's because of sandbanks and his fear of smashing into one. If we run aground it could be days before anyone could pull us off,' Ronaldo pointed out.

'I doubt this old tub would cope very well; she might end up with a big hole below the water line!' Tim warned.

'Let's just pray he gets the engines working again. This is one of the worst storms I've been caught up in for a long time,' Ronaldo yelled, his comments almost lost in a crack of thunder.

'I don't want to be rescued in the Amazon again!' Tim shouted to his friend with a broad grin.

After another twenty minutes or so the storm died down, but there was still no sign of the big diesel engines starting up again. From the lights coming from the villages on the banks the boys could see that the vessel was indeed drifting downstream and it was impossible to tell how close to the bank the boat was travelling. The captain had positioned extra lookouts so he could try and direct the ship, but without power it was a difficult task. The boat and all the passengers were now at the mercy of the river current.

Suddenly there was a terrific jolt! Some of the passengers were tipped out of their hammocks. Ronaldo fell over Tim and landed on top of a crate of chickens. The young doc helped up his friend. The hens were surprisingly quiet and on closer inspection Ronaldo discovered why; they were all dead from fright and the soaking they had suffered in the thunderstorm.

'Sandbank?' Tim asked.

'Yes, let's hope it's just a little one!' Ronaldo replied.

Nimrod II was stuck and seriously so. Fortunately the crew had managed to get the generator working so the vessel was now well lit; the other great fear was that another riverboat would come round the corner and plough straight into them, as had happened in the past on the Tigre, with great loss of life.

A couple of passengers had been injured: a little girl had been thrown out of her hammock and hurt her shoulder and a middle-aged woman had a bad cut to her head. Tim was able to put his casualty skills to work. He examined the child and found her to have a broken collar bone; the doc applied a suitable bandage and advised her mother that she would be as good as new in few weeks. The older patient needed nine stitches which Tim very efficiently and neatly inserted, watched by a hushed group of fellow passengers.

At first light the position of the vessel was fully realised. She had lodged firmly onto a large sandbank on one of the many twists of the Tigre and her bow had swung round to face the east bank of the river. The boat had come to rest about fifty metres opposite the village of Berlin, Nimrod II's last port of call; most of the community's inhabitants stood on the bank watching, the children squatting in their usual pose waiting to see what was going to happen next.

'If he can't restart those engines this boat is going to be here for an awful long time,' Tim said to his friend. 'Did you say that village is called Berlin? Have you heard of the city of Berlin in Germany?'

'No, I haven't heard of any other Berlin. Another in Germany, that's in Europe isn't it?' Ronaldo queried.

'Yeah, that's correct; it's the capital of Germany. How far are we from Intuto?' Tim asked his friend, wondering if he would ever make it to Nueva Casa.

'About nine hours in a fast boat, or a day and a half in a canoe if powered by the small pecky-pecky engines,' Ronaldo reckoned, after a bit of thought.

'I don't suppose there'll be any fast boats in Berlin will there?' Tim asked.

'Not much chance,' Ronaldo laughed. 'There might be a couple of big canoes with pecky-pecky engines, that's all.'

Just after midday the engines began to cough and splutter into action. Billows of dark diesel smoke poured from its exhausts, making anyone near choke with the acrid fumes. A loud cheer went up from the passengers and then the moment they had all been waiting for, the loud roar of full reverse throttle. The ship shuddered but wouldn't budge. The captain tried again and again, but the water around the ship only became muddier as the propellers churned up the sand beneath them.

The captain repeated the whole exercise an hour later but again without success. Word went round the vessel from the captain that he would need another ship to pull Nimrod II off the sandbank and he estimated it would be a few days before help would arrive. His advice was to finish the journey by small boat.

Soon a small flotilla of canoes arrived from Berlin to take the passengers ashore. Tim and Ronaldo agreed that the best plan would be to join one of the big canoes heading north to Intuto at first light. A night in the jungle en route could be a bit rough Tim thought, but then being stranded in the middle of the river eaten by mosquitoes wasn't much fun either. At least this way he would get to Nueva Casa within the next couple of days whereas it was now doubtful if Nimrod II would ever reach its intended destination.

———◆———

'Look Tim, there're lights up ahead,' Ronaldo shouted to his friend above the noise of the pecky-pecky engine. 'It should be Intuto!'

'Thank you God! I thought we weren't going to make it,' Tim confided in his friend. 'The last few hours perched on the side of this overloaded canoe, with all these people, was almost too much for me. I was sure we were going to hit a log and be tipped into the river. If we were lucky we would have made it to shore downstream but my entire medical gear would have been lost.'

'Oh man! Where's your faith? God didn't bring you this far just to feed you to the camen! You've got lives to save!' Ronaldo said, as slapped his friend on the back. Ronaldo was just as pleased as Tim to be approaching Intuto jetty. He had been praying hard ever since darkness fell; he knew just how dangerous these waters could be after dark.

'Do you think the message we sent from Berlin will have reached Miguel?' Tim asked. 'I suppose time will tell; if not we'll have to find somewhere to spend the night in the village. I just want to get off this boat and away from these mosquitoes. Not sure I'll be able to sit down for days!'

Five minutes later and they were standing on the wooden jetty of the small remote regional town at the top of the Rio Tigre, the furthest point the riverboats reached. Tim rubbed his aching backside and legs. It was around ten o'clock at night yet still there were lots of townspeople about. But there was no sign of Miguel.

'So where are we going to now, Ronaldo? Who will let these travellers rest their weary heads?' Tim asked his friend, obviously fed up that he still hadn't yet arrived at his destination.

Before Ronaldo could answer a young man came running down the jetty towards them ... it was Miguel! The three men embraced, thrilled to be together again. Miguel explained that Nuevo Casa was about half an hour away by canoe. He realised that Ronaldo and Tim were exhausted after their thirty-six hour boat trip and in no mood to set foot in another canoe, so the three decided to spend the night in Intuto. Tim was glad, especially as Miguel promised to show him the medical centre in the morning.

The next morning Tim was looking forward to his tour of the clinic. He was shown round by Victor, the caretaker, as there were no medical staff in the town. There was a nurse but he was up river, near the Ecuador border; he had gone to the communities there to immunise the new babies. The pharmacy door was locked but the caretaker had an inventory for Tim to look over. The young doctor wasn't impressed: a few antibiotics, paracetamol and some anti-malaria doses. Tim was then taken to the labour ward which looked as if it could do with a good scrub. The walls had been white-washed once upon a time but now they were greyish, with crumbling cement and mould growing in the corners. The birthing bed was a rusty iron object in the centre of the room covered by a torn, rubber mattress, with stuffing hanging from it. A small crib lay on a shelf underneath the windowsill; the thin mattress looked filthy too. Not the best place to enter the world Tim thought. They moved on to the operating room, the sight of which sent a shudder down his spine; it was so basic he almost wept. There was rubbish on the floor, old blood-soaked dressings, dirty plastic bottles under the sink. The smell was musty and awful.

'Please God don't ask me to do any surgery in this place,' he muttered to himself raising baffled looks from the caretaker.

'That's fine, now show me the rest of the place,' he said to his guide as he cleared his throat.

His tour complete, Tim walked down to the jetty to join the others; Miguel and Ronaldo had been gathering some supplies for the village. On the other side of the jetty, Tim spotted a high-powered speedboat unlike any he had seen on the Rio Tigre before. Before he could ask Miguel about it, four big guys in jungle fatigues walked quickly towards the vessel. The man at the back of the group gave Tim a suspicious glance which made the young doc feel very uneasy. Within minutes the fast boat was fired up and away upstream towards the north.

'Who were those guys? I wouldn't like to pick a fight with any of them!' Tim remarked.

'They've been coming for supplies for a few weeks now. Some think they're prospecting for gold, others wonder if they're into cocaine smuggling; they never seemed to be armed but I wouldn't want to mess with them,' Miguel replied.

'They won't carry weapons openly, with all the army activity around here, but who knows what's under their shirts!' Ronaldo chipped in.

'Never mind them, let's get going. There are lots of sick kids for Tim to see,' Miguel said, as he pulled the cord to start the pecky-pecky engine.

Chapter 5

Savaged

A couple of days later the student journalist was sent out on her own again. Information had arrived at the news desk that a five-year-old boy had been mauled by a dog in the local park. The child had been taken to hospital but his condition was unknown. Katie was the only 'reporter' still in the building so Sandra despatched the trainee to the hospital to find out the story.

When Katie arrived there was already a small crowd of five reporters and a radio crew hanging around. The 'word' was that a hospital spokesman was going to address the group shortly.

Sure enough about ten minutes later a stocky man of about fifty years, dressed smartly in a grey suit appeared; he looked in sombre mood. He was accompanied by a female police inspector.

'I have been instructed by the parents of Darren Flett to inform you that their son has suffered very serious injuries to his face and neck. He is currently undergoing emergency surgery to stabilise his condition but it is anticipated that he will be transferred to Great Ormond Street Children's Hospital for further treatment as soon as it is safe to do so.'

'Do we know anything about the dog? What breed of dog was responsible? Has the dog been destroyed?' one of the reporters called out from the throng.

The policewoman took the question, 'This was a very serious incident; a young boy has been severely mauled. The dog was a terrier, breed yet to be confirmed; the animal posed a significant risk to the public and my officers, so it has been shot by a marksman.'

'Has the owner been identified?' a young woman's voice asked from the crowd of reporters. The unfamiliar tones caused the regular media folk to look round to identify the source. Katie had just taken her courage in both hands.

'Not as yet but our enquiries continue,' the inspector answered. 'That's all for the moment. Thank you.'

Katie was appalled: it sounded as if the poor boy was very badly injured. The young reporter hurried back to the office but there was no sign of Sandra. She spied Alf, but he had no idea where the editor might be. Katie decided to discuss the incident with him as it was already evident this was going to be a big story; she had seen a BBC satellite truck heading for the hospital so the incident would go national.

Alf listened intently then said 'You write the preliminary report for Sandra but I'll take over now. Be sure to email a copy to me. Which hospital did you say? Did you get the name of the inspector?'

'It's the hospital off North Street. I didn't get the inspector's name.'

'You're meant to be a reporter! You must always get the name, occupation or rank of anyone you get a story from. It's fundamental, young woman!' Alf said sternly.

'Oops! Sorry.'

'Details are everything to a journalist. Which park was it?'

'Crawford Park in Westfield.'

'Good! At least you managed to get some information,' Alf replied sarcastically. 'That'll be Juniper Road police station; I'll give the press officer a phone and see if there's an update. You'd better get cracking on the report for Sandra; she'll be back soon.'

Katie walked over to her desk doubting her abilities again, but after a couple of minutes she snapped out of her self-pity. She knew she could be a journalist; she just had to keep trying and keep learning. Besides, she did have a lot of valuable information and she was going to prove it by writing a good report. Alf had really riled her; she was determined to prove him wrong.

As she wrote her piece she couldn't get the poor boy out of her mind. What a frightening experience for him and what about his parents; they must be distraught, poor people. The child would probably be disfigured for life, if he survived and even that sounded touch and go, she thought.

Sandra came into the office just as Katie was checking through her work.

'Katie, how did you get on? Did you find out what happened to the boy at the hospital? The local radio has picked up on the story too. Have you managed to speak to the parents yet?'

Before Katie could reply Alf was at Sandra's side.

'I have managed to make contact with the father,' he said. 'We have an exclusive. I'm going to meet him at the hospital in ten minutes. Oh, the boy is still in surgery.'

'Great! Get to it. We'll run it tomorrow. Take Katie with you,' Sandra instructed, as she dashed out of the door.

'Come on kid, let's see if we can teach you something,' Alf shouted across the office.

The young student grabbed her jacket and ran after the journalist. Alf knew his way around the hospital so within minutes of arrival in the building they were sitting waiting in the main foyer. Katie couldn't believe that a father would want to speak to a reporter while his son was in surgery.

'How did you manage to make contact with the father?' she asked Alf.

'I was given his mobile number by a friend of mine.'

'So you phoned him up, while his son was in surgery, and asked to interview him?' Katie asked incredulously. She couldn't believe anyone would be so callous.

'Yip. Mr Flett is a very angry man; he wants the world to know what happened to his son and who's responsible. Here he comes now,' Alf replied, nodding in the direction of a young man dressed in a blue boiler suit.

The group moved into a corner of the hospital café, a more private spot. Jim Flett was emotional, both a caring, distraught father and a very angry man. He explained he had not seen the incident, as he had been at work, but that he knew from his wife what had happened.

Three youths, presumably from the nearby estate, had been walking through the park with what looked like a pit bull terrier. Kelly, his wife, and Darren were about a hundred metres from the pond; Darren had a small bag of bread crumbs to feed to the ducks. Kelly had spotted the lads, with the dog on its lead, about twenty metres away. Their odd behaviour had attracted her attention; they were staggering and shoving each other. She assumed they were high on drugs so hurried past them to the pond. When they reached the pond Darren started to throw bread to the ducks, as he always did. Without warning the dog pounced on him and tossed him to the ground.

Jim became tearful, ringing his hands as he relayed the next part of the attack. Kelly had told him that the dog treated Darren like a rag doll, shaking him and tossing him in the air. Jim said Darren would have been killed if it hadn't been for the quick thinking of one of the park's gardeners; this young woman grabbed her rake and ran screaming towards the dog. Fearlessly she hit the animal with her implement drawing blood from its back. The dog lost interest in Darren and dropped him in a heap before it attacked the gardener. When Kelly got to the boy he was bleeding heavily and silent.

Katie began to feel unwell; she thought she was going to be sick. She excused herself and headed for the ladies. There she slumped on the floor, feeling awful. It took the student ten minutes or more to regain her composure and by the time she returned Jim had left.

'Are you alright girl?' Alf asked sympathetically. 'I'm glad you left, I thought you were going to keel over.'

'I'm fine now, thanks. That was terrible! That poor boy! Where's Jim?'

'A nurse from the Intensive Care Unit came for him,' Alf explained. 'You'll need to control your emotions. What would have happened if you had been on your own?'

'What happened to the gardener? Did she get hurt?' Katie asked, as she tried to find out the rest of the story.

'No. The head gardener was working in the same flower bed but slightly further back. He had a spade in his hand. Wham! The dog took off, yelping as it went, into the woods at the back of the park.'

'What about those boys, did the police arrest them?'

'According to Jim they were so 'stoned' they didn't even try to pull the dog off or runaway. They just sat on the grass as if nothing had happened; when the police arrived they were immediately arrested. After a half hour search, a police marksman found the dog in the woods and shot it. If the boy dies they'll be done for manslaughter!'

'Oh don't say that, surely he'll survive,' Katie replied, coughing gently to hide the emotion in her voice.

'From the look on the nurse's face, I would say it's not looking good,' Alf commented. 'You go back to the office and bring Sandra "up to speed". I'll hang around here for a while and see if we get any updates.'

Katie was happy to get out of the hospital. Unlike her brother she couldn't stand anything to do with needles and clinics. She habitually fainted if she was given a jab or had a blood test. Tim on the other hand had always loved to watch medical programmes on the television, he was just fascinated.

The young reporter met with her editor and updated her as instructed.

———◆———

Just before five in the afternoon, Alf returned to the office with the sad news that Darren had not survived. The seasoned journalist then sat down at his desk and typed up the story for the morning paper, without a hint of emotion. Katie couldn't believe his seemingly hard heart; she was stunned and had to fight back the tears.

Alf looked up from his keyboard and commented in his usual gruff way, 'You'll have to toughen up lass. If you're going to be a journalist there'll be many more Darrens so you can't allow it to get personal.'

Grateful it was time to go home Katie grabbed her jacket and bolted out the door.

———◦———

In the evening after a hot bath, Katie relaxed on her settee and thought over the day. She was so aware of the tragedy that had just fallen on the Flett family: the parents, the siblings and the grandparents, their lives would never be the same without their little boy. Katie realised that Darren's classmates would hear what happened to their friend and be very, very sad. People watching the news or reading the newspaper would be upset by the shocking news too.

The student wondered why it always seemed to be the young innocents who suffered; Darren was just feeding the ducks, a terrible waste of a young life. Katie managed to choke back her tears. She acknowledged that Alf was right: she needed to control her emotions or she would never make it as a journalist.

Chapter 6

Time to Work

Nueva Casa was a typical Amazonian village of around twenty houses, perched on the banks of the river. The homes, with palm leaf roofs and floors raised about a metre off the ground, were set in a traditional rectangle around an open grassed area. The group arrived around midday to a wonderful reception from the village folks. Young men clambered down the steep banks of the Waldoo River to carry Tim's bags to his hut. They had built a brand new house for their highly respected guest; Tim was shocked that they had gone to such lengths for him. His memory of village life was jogged by the aroma coming from the cooking pots and the wood smoke as it blew across the community.

'I was expecting a corner in a hut with the other young men,' Tim said to Miguel.

'Many of my people remember the young gringo and his sister who lived with them all those years ago. Here's Raul! You and he used to go hunting with Ronaldo. Do you remember him?' Miguel asked, as a short, stocky lad with a huge grin walked over to join them.

'I certainly do! Who could forget a grin like Raul's?' Tim

said as he reached to embrace his old friend. Raul had huge muscles compared to Tim, both in his arms and legs, but it was obvious that the hunter couldn't believe how tall Tim was; Raul kept looking the village guest up and down in astonishment!

Other young men queued up to welcome Tim, some with very familiar yet manly faces now, but no names came to mind. The young medic wished he could remember more names but in truth he never thought he would see these people again; after all he and Katie had sneaked away, under the cover of darkness, to escape to Iquitos all those years ago.

'These guys built your house; they volunteered. Don't get too carried away, my friend, because you'll have to share with Ronaldo while he's here and of course any patients you might have; this is your clinic too!' Miguel added with a huge smile. 'But look there's a screen in the back corner; you can sling your hammock there. At least you'll have a little space to call your own.'

The three men walked around the clinic. Tim was so impressed that the villagers had thought about him and had wanted to make him feel at home. Just as they were leaving the clinic to have a tour of the community, Raul came up and whispered in Miguel's ear.

'Raul wants to know, when will you start seeing the sick?' Miguel asked, 'His four-year-old daughter has fever.'

'After you've seen the children, please come with me to see Chief Bruno; he's too sick to come to you.'

'Of course I'll check on Bruno, in about an hour. I'll start here as soon as I have unpacked a few things. Tell Raul to spread the word round the village. Oh! I could do with a table and a chair to work from if possible,' Tim requested, as he turned to go indoors to prepare for his first patients.

Within ten minutes Tim had a line of about thirty villagers sitting patiently outside his hut. This was his first clinic, on his own, ever. He had usually worked as part of a team so always had a senior doctor to turn to, but he was on his own now!

The rest of the day flew by. Most of the children he saw had a diarrhoeal illness, probably from the dirty water; some were dehydrated and desperately in need of fluids. Tim had a good supply of rehydration salts but he knew that for the future he would have to think of ways to educate the parents on how to care for their sick children. One or two had high fever, which in the tropics was malaria until proven otherwise. Tim asked Miguel to take these children to Intuto in the evening, by then the nurse would have returned. The nurse had a malaria testing kit which was issued by the government. Miguel wasn't keen to travel to the town in the dark but Tim insisted; some of the children were quite unwell and needed treatment as soon as possible.

Tim was grateful that although there was currently no doctor in this provincial town, the government had ensured there was a nurse who had been trained to assess and treat malaria. By providing this essential service the Ministry of Health made at least some attempt to limit the effects of the deadly mosquito. The nurse should be able to diagnose the type of malaria and give the correct tablets. As yet, Tim wasn't sure he was skilled enough to look at a drop of a patient's blood under the microscope and decide which type of malaria he was dealing with. He was confident he would recognise the malaria bug, as he had learnt to do this while in Papua New Guinea, but which form of the disease and therefore which treatment to use was another matter.

Once the clinic was finished Miguel arrived to take Tim to see Bruno, who only the day before had installed Miguel as the new chief. He was lying on a mat on the floor with his wife by his side. He managed a smile for Tim and gingerly stretched out his hand to him. The young doctor could see his patient had lost a lot of weight; his eyes were deeply yellow and he had many bruises on his skin, all of which indicated to Tim that his liver had failed and that he probably had a cancer. Tim examined Bruno's abdomen to find a huge craggy lump which confirmed his diagnosis. Tim looked in his eyes and could tell that the chief already knew he wasn't long for this life.

About an hour later, one of the hunters returned with a machete wound to his leg. Marco was carried in by one of the other men and placed on the table. The tribesmen had tried to stop the bleeding with a bundle of leaves tied in place with a bit of rope. Tim carefully removed the 'dressing' to reveal a ten centimetre, deep cut on the man's right shin.

Ronaldo stayed with Tim to help with any dialect problems he might encounter. Although Tim's Spanish was excellent, many of the villagers preferred to speak in their own local language even though they did have a grasp of Spanish from their primary school days.

'He did this while he was hacking through the jungle to take a look at the new mining works,' Ronaldo reported.

'What mining? Miguel didn't mention any mining round here,' Tim said slightly puzzled.

'The exploration started earlier this year. The workers

have cut down a large area of trees so the men of the village are worried that the animals will be scared off and there will be no hunting,' Ronaldo continued.

'How far away are they working?'

'It's about two kilometres upstream from here. They are not a very friendly bunch; the first time our men went to have a look they went by canoe but they were chased off by armed guards,' Ronaldo explained, as he peered over the victim's wound.

'Tell him I'll have to put some stitches in his leg. A lot of stitches! But he's lucky as I have some local anaesthetic,' Tim instructed, while searching for the ampule of anaesthetic in his drug box.

'What's "local anaesth …"?' his friend enquired still staring at the cut leg, watching the blood trickle slowly onto the dirt floor of the hut.

'Sorry! It's a sort of painkiller, it'll make his leg go numb; he won't feel the stitches go in,' Tim explained, handing some gauze to Ronaldo. 'Here do something useful; hold this pad firmly over the wound until we get the bleeding stopped completely.'

After about twenty minutes of cleaning and suturing the wound was sewn together and dressed. Marco was very grateful to Tim, shaking his hand profusely before he left the clinic.

'What are they mining? Do you know?' Tim asked Ronaldo, as they made there way across to Miguel's hut for some food.

'I'm not too sure; some say gold, others oil. Maybe Miguel knows more now,' Ronaldo offered.

The men folk of the village had gathered in the headman's hut and were discussing the mining when Tim and

Ronaldo arrived. Marco was showing off his 'war' wound and his pristine bandage. The hunters' discussions became quite heated with lots of gesticulation and some very angry outbursts but Tim couldn't understand what they were saying though he knew the mining issue was a big problem for them.

Ronaldo explained the situation to Tim after the men folk had returned to their huts for a siesta.

'It's oil. The drillers have made a huge mess there already, destroying many trees. During the rainy season they brought heavy machinery upstream on barges. Most days fast boats, carrying workers, speed past Nueva Casa. The miners have built a settlement big enough for about one hundred people and so far they have destroyed about ten hectares of forest. Since they arrived in the area the number of dead fish in the river has risen some tenfold, which is another great worry for the community here.'

Miguel nodded in agreement as Ronaldo continued to update Tim on the current situation.

'The Peruvian government in Lima has granted licences to many oil companies to explore large areas of the western Amazon. Local tribal leaders have been fighting hard to stop it but without success. There were big demonstrations in Moyobama by the local people last year, but it ended with four villagers being killed in the riot that followed.'

Miguel added, 'There are supposed to be state controls to protect the environment and the local people, but often they're ignored. It's all about money and not for poor villagers like us. No one seems to remember or care that our tribes have lived in the rainforest for hundreds of years. That's why the men are so upset.'

Tim could see that the brothers were indeed deeply

troubled by the rate of change that was occurring in the rainforest and the impact it was having on the indigenous peoples, but he felt powerless to help them despite agreeing with their point of view.

Just before Miguel was due to set off for Intuto with the children, he divulged to Tim and Ronaldo another worrying development that had occurred since he had arrived in Nueva Casa. The army had stopped a shipment of cocaine on the Rio Tigre, just south of Intuto. There had been a firefight and two of the soldiers were killed as well as all of the smugglers. Miguel admitted that he was really disturbed by this as it meant that the drug barons were working to the north of Intuto, close to the Ecuador border. The new chief knew only too well of the brutality of these people; he and his community had been so badly terrorised by the cocaine gangs at the time of Tim and Katie's plane crash.

Miguel stared at the glowing embers of the fire, deep in thought as he relived those terrible moments when the gang entered his home village: the gunfire, the shouts of abuse, the screaming, and the fear of his people. Tim attempted to relieve his friend's anguish and inject some hope into the conversation.

'Maybe the soldiers killed them all in the skirmish on the river?' he suggested.

'No chance! These barons never do their own deliveries. They have "monkeys" for that sort of work. Remember the strangers we saw in Intuto as we left? They weren't miners. Did you see their hands? Those hands haven't laboured in anything to do with mines, or oil,' Miguel declared, as he drew aimlessly with a stick on the dusty mud floor.

'At least Nueva Casa is not on the Rio Tigre. They won't bother us up here on the Rio Waldoo. We're too small for them, not enough young men for any sort of labour force,' Ronaldo offered, as he too tried to calm his brother's fears.

'I wished I shared your optimism little brother. I hope you're right,' Miguel replied, standing up to go to the canoes.

As they were talking, José, one of the young men rushed in looking for Tim. He spoke very quickly in his own dialect to Miguel so Tim couldn't follow his story, but he knew something really serious had happened, possibly life threatening by the look of deep anxiety on the man's face.

'What is it?' Tim asked, a feeling of apprehension beginning to grip him as well.

'José's six-year-old son was in the forest with his friends when he was attacked by a swarm of bees. He was stung several times and now he is swelling up and having difficulty breathing,' Ronaldo explained, as swiftly as he could.

'Anaphylaxis!' Tim thought out loud. 'Tell him to bring the child to the clinic straightaway.'

Both Tim and Ronaldo rushed to the clinic while José went to collect his child. Tim reminded himself of the dose of adrenalin for a six year old as he ran across the grass to the clinic; he knew that if he was right and this was a serious allergic reaction then every second counted. The young doctor reached for his medical pack and pulled out the allergy kit box. He searched carefully for an ampoule of adrenalin. Quickly he drew up the correct dose for a young child and checked it against the dose chart that he had carefully attached to the lid of the box before leaving the UK. He knew how easy it was to muddle doses in an emergency and he didn't want to run the risk of doing so.

José arrived with his boy, Pedro. He looked dreadful: his face was swollen, lips blue and his body covered with red blotches. Tim knew just by looking at Pedro that he stood between the boy and certain death.

Tim leaned over the boy and injected the adrenalin into the youngster's thigh; he watched anxiously as the boy fought for life with each laboured breath he took. Tim beckoned to the father to come over and stroke his son's brow, to speak to the child to try and stop him falling into unconsciousness.

The doctor checked his watch, if there was no improvement in five minutes he would have to give the boy another dose. Tim knew that too big a dose was very dangerous to the heart, but he also knew that he would have to take the risk otherwise the child would not survive.

Two minutes and still the boy's face was deep pink and swollen, his breathing still very rapid and noisy. Tim wished he had a nebuliser and some oxygen to relieve the child's distress.

'Come on drug, work!' Tim muttered, under his breath.

By now Miguel and some of the other elders of the village had arrived to watch the scene. The witch doctor sneaked in the back, even though he knew that Tim had no time for his magic, as on their first meeting, Tim had told the shaman to stay well away from the clinic. Miguel, also a man of faith, understood Tim's viewpoint and must have read the medic's mind because he signalled to two of his hunters to escort the witch doctor from the hut. But the shaman was very unhappy at his ejection and shouted abusive things to José. Miguel, as the chief, was the only one in the village who could dictate to the shaman and Tim was really glad that his friend was there.

Soon the five minutes were up. Tim could feel his own pulse rising as he contemplated his next decision. He had drawn up another dose of adrenalin and knew he would have to give it as Pedro's condition was no better. In truth Tim had never treated an anaphylaxis before. When he was a medical student attached to Accident and Emergency, a teenager had come in with a peanut allergy but that lad had responded with the first dose. Resuscitation equipment was available then too: oxygen, nebulisers, and intravenous drips, so he definitely stood a better chance. If Pedro didn't respond to this next dose then …

Within three minutes of the second injection Pedro's breathing seemed less laboured. Tim listened to the boy's chest with his stethoscope to check his heart rate, and to his delight the beats were slowing down, just slightly; there were fewer wheezes and squeaks in his lungs as well. The boy's colour was improving, his lips less swollen … yes, his treatment had worked! Pedro was on the mend.

Twenty minutes later and the smile on José's face said it all as he cradled his son in his arms. Pedro was now able to sip water and was wondering what all the fuss was about. His only complaint was of an itchy chin and face but much to Tim's satisfaction the swelling around the boy's face and neck had subsided greatly. José's wife, Andrea, came running into the clinic; she had been in Intuto with some of the others buying provisions and had just arrived home. Tim assessed Andrea was about six months pregnant, but she still managed to take her son onto her lap as she listened to the whole story. Soon, she too, was grinning with delight at the happy outcome.

Once everyone dispersed back to their homes Tim flopped into his hammock exhausted from the stress of treating the child. He quietly thanked God for helping him save Pedro's life. Later in the evening José and Andrea came back bearing fruits that José had gathered especially for Tim. It was obvious that José had a story to tell Tim so when Ronaldo arrived he translated a most interesting tale.

José remembered that when he was a child his younger sister, Clara, had been in the forest with her friends gathering fruits. One evening she was brought home by the older children, screaming. She had been stung by bees as well. José described the same swelling, difficulty breathing and blotches all over her body. The shaman came and danced around her and rubbed potion on her head but within an hour she was dead. Now, Tim understood why José had been so terrified when he came running to find him that afternoon; he knew that Pedro could have died and that Tim was the only hope.

Pedro made a full recovery over the next few days, but Tim still kept a close eye on him. His parents were advised, if at all possible, to keep him well away from bees. Tim wondered what would happen should the boy be stung again after Tim was gone. Back home he knew parents would be issued with an Epipen, a single use syringe with a dose of adrenalin, ready to be injected into the thigh muscle should the child be stung by a bee. Would he be able to get a supply for Pedro? Would it keep in these temperatures? Tim decided he would have to look into this when he returned to Iquitos because it might just save Pedro's life should he be stung again.

Three days later Miguel received a radio message from the mayor of Intuto. A twenty-year-old man had fallen off a roof he was repairing and had hit his head on a boulder. He was knocked out for about ten minutes then seemed to recover, although he had a bit of a headache. But half an hour later, he started to vomit and complained of a severe headache. Within ten minutes he became unconscious again, but this time his wife couldn't wake him. Would Dr Tim please come and help him?

Miguel rushed to find Tim and told him the story.

'The mayor is asking for your help because he has heard of your successful treatment of Pedro! Will you go?' Miguel asked his friend, hoping he would agree.

'Of course I'll go but I'm no neurosurgeon. It sounds as if this guy needs airlifted to hospital,' Tim suggested, already considering what he could possibly do for the man if he had a severe head injury.

'We both know that's never going to happen. Not one family in Intuto can afford the riverboat fare to Iquitos never mind the services of a brain surgeon,' Miguel remarked, almost laughing. 'Come, I'll take you in my canoe. Let's go.'

'Great, I'll get my medic bag, just give me two secs,' Tim said, as he scampered around the clinic gathering up his equipment.

The trip into Intuto was much quicker than the outward journey as they canoed with the current. As on the first night there were strangers hanging about the jetty. Even Tim could tell they didn't look like locals; their features were subtly different and their body language said 'don't mess with me'. Tim picked up Miguel's unease as the two hurried past. The young gringo could feel the eyes of the men drill into his back as he walked briskly up the slope to the town.

'Who are those guys?' Tim asked, once they were out of earshot.

'I don't know, but they don't belong here. They make me feel very nervous and I didn't like the way they looked at you. You'd think they had never seen a gringo before,' Miguel remarked, as they opened the door to the clinic.

The doctor found his patient lying on his back on a bashed up trolley. Tim quickly and carefully moved the casualty onto his side to protect his windpipe in case he vomited and fluids ended up in his lungs. Tim then began to assess the young man before he removed the scrappy piece of cloth covering his wound. The patient whose name was Ernesto was breathing normally but he was unconscious; he didn't respond to a command, but when Tim rubbed on his chest bone he did react. Tim checked his pupils; his right pupil was dilated and responding very slowly to light whereas his left pupil was small and normal.

'He must have bleeding inside his skull. The story is classic: head injury, patient knocked out, initially recovers and then slips back into unconsciousness,' Tim pronounced, but as he went over the history again in his mind he came to the awful realisation that he would have to do something and quickly.

'Can you do anything?' the mayor asked. 'He's my son-in-law, the father of six of my grandchildren.'

Tim looked up and saw the children, plus Ernesto's wife, watching him with frightened eyes from the back of the room.

'I'll do my best. But we'll need to get everyone outside. Is the nurse around?' Tim asked the mayor.

'He's through in the back searching for dressings; he'll be here in a minute,' the mayor quickly replied.

A few minutes later a young thin man in his mid-twenties walked through carrying some dressings.

'Hello, I'm Federico. You must be Dr Tim?' the nurse said, as he stretched out his hand. 'I've heard you are a very good doctor.'

'I do my best. Have you looked at this man?' Tim asked, hoping for some other clinical input.

'Only his head wound; I've found some bandages,' Federico replied. 'He's in a bad way.'

'He'll need more than dressings. What surgical equipment do we have?' Tim asked.

'Not much; some basics for abdominal surgery. I've only been here a few days so I haven't had the chance to search round everything. Come with me and we can look together,' the nurse suggested.

The pair disappeared off to the locked dispensary where everything was kept secure. Federico found a box containing surgical instruments but it only contained scalpels, forceps and retractors, the most commonly used operating tools.

'Surely there's more than this? I need something to make a hole in his skull and I need it now! This man is going to die if we don't act fast,' Tim shouted, anxiously.

'Here doctor, there's another box down on the bottom shelf,' Federico called out, from the floor at the back of the cupboard that served as the dispensary.

Quickly the two young men opened up the container. There were lots of different pieces of surgical equipment that Tim didn't recognise, but again not what he was looking for. Just as he stood up, a bashed-up metal box with English writing on the outside caught his eye. He could make out the words 'Hand tools' but not much else. The doctor opened up the box and found just what he needed – a drill.

'This'll do the trick. Now all we need to do is clean up the drill bit. Federico you go and sterilise it while I check on Ernesto,' Tim instructed, as he rushed back through to his patient.

They had only been gone ten minutes but Tim could see worrying changes in Ernesto. He was more deeply unconscious; his breathing had changed for the worse, Tim shouted for Federico.

'We have to do this now! Help me roll him onto his side. Bring the razor so we can remove the hair above his temple,' Tim asserted, adrenalin now coursing round his veins. 'Where is the antiseptic to clean the area?'

'Here, Dr Tim, I have everything for you now,' Federico replied, slowly, trying to calm the situation a little. He was astute enough to realise that his young doctor was way out of his comfort zone.

The young medics worked hard and within three minutes Tim was ready. He stood over Ernesto with the drill in his hand, 'Oh God please let us find a blood clot and save this man,' he prayed quietly.

Tim placed the bit of the drill onto the patient's skull bone and gently turned the handle. At first he was making no impression because he was being so cautious.

'Press a little harder Tim,' Federico said, gently encouraging his doctor.

The bit was beginning to bite into the bone, slowly going deeper, then the resistance gave way, but Tim was ready for it, preventing the end of the drill pushing into the brain. Out came the blood through the burr hole to Tim and Federico's delight. But after a while the blood stopped flowing and Tim knew he had to make another hole about two centimetres away from the original one. This was more successful with a greater amount of blood escaping which released some of the pressure on Ernesto's brain.

Tim was watching and waiting wondering if he should make yet another hole in the skull when Ernesto started to have an epileptic fit.

'We need to give him some intravenous diazepam to stop this fit,' Tim said, urgently, to Federico.

The nurse quickly handed Tim the vial; he drew up the correct dose and slowly injected the calming medicine into Ernesto's vein.

'This is a bad sign; he must have damage deep in his brain as well as the clot under his skull,' Tim said, feeling down-hearted. 'There's no more I can do for him, we'll just have to wait and see.'

The diazepam stopped Ernesto's fit but his condition continued to deteriorate.

'Shall I bring in Ernesto's wife?' Federico asked; he too had recognised that the patient was not going to make it.

'Yes, of course,' Tim said, softly.

Tim had noted Ernesto's change of posture, his head was extended back and his hands were now in the posture of someone with irretrievable brain damage.

Ernesto died twenty minutes later with his family beside him. Tim was distraught, if only he could have done more. But even he realised that the most sophisticated of neuro-surgical wards would have had difficulty saving Ernesto with bleeding deep in his brain. Tim had released the pressure from the clot under the skull so he had done all he could, but still he felt bad.

Chapter 7

Secrets

Monday morning of the fourth and final week; Katie mulled over the previous three weeks as she munched her muesli. The attachment had just flown by and as promised the editor, Sandra, had kept her really busy; Katie realised that she had learnt a lot. Alf had been a real help to her; disinterested in the student to start with and obviously a reluctant tutor, he warmed to the young woman because of her tenacity and determination to always give of her best.

There had been interesting stories to follow up, some were pretty mundane but with each she felt that a different aspect of journalistic art had been explored. Sandra hadn't turned out to be 'the dragon' Katie had been warned about but she certainly exacted high standards.

Katie felt that she had hardened up a little too; she believed she had better control of her emotions, at least in public. She knew that at times she still became very upset and angry at some of the stories she covered, like the elderly couple who had been beaten senseless by two drug addicts who had broken into their home. The eighty year old's house had been ransacked and everything precious to them destroyed. Katie had interviewed the couple in hospital during their convalescence and she could see how badly injured they had been. She knew that the elderly were often victims of robbery because their frailty made them easy prey for drug addicts; good sources of cash for their next fix. Katie began to feel incensed as she realised, that as in the death of Darren, drug addiction had found yet more victims.

The seven o'clock news interrupted the trainee's reflections; she gulped down the last of her coffee and cleared away her breakfast dishes. Let's hope nothing drastic happens this week Katie thought, as she gathered together her car keys and jacket and rushed out of her flat.

'Hi Katie, how are you this bright and beautiful morning? I've got a strange one for you. We've had an email from a woman living in Dorwood; she says she has a story but she only wants to speak to a female reporter,' John declared, as he walked over to Katie.

'Why does it have to be a female reporter? How do I get in touch with her?' Katie asked, curiously.

'She left her phone number so I rang her a minute ago to get the 'lowdown' but she insisted she would only talk to a woman. You, Katie, are the only woman in the office today; Sandra is at a meeting up in London and Jackie and Chloe are on holiday. So it's over to you,' John explained.

'I wonder what it could be about. It seems a strange request.'

'Oh, don't worry; it's probably to discuss the closure of the public toilets on Mains Street. Women don't like to talk to guys about such things!' John said, with a cheeky look in his eye.

'Where does she live?'

'Oh! I forgot to say. She doesn't want you to go to her house but to meet in the café opposite the cathedral.'

'Where does she live anyway? Is it in the smart part of town or in one of the estates?' Katie asked, trying to gather some more information on her new case.

'I dunno, she wouldn't say. I'm a guy remember. You'll be fine, it's a busy enough café, so don't get freaked.'

'It's cool. No problem. When am I supposed to meet her?'

'I'll forward the email to you; you can sort it out.'

At three o'clock that afternoon Katie arrived at the café. It was a gorgeous sunny day so after looking around inside to check there was no one matching the description she'd been given, Katie ordered a mineral water and sat outside. Ten minutes went by, then another ten; the young reporter was beginning to get restless and thought she had been stood up when a car pulled into the parking area next to the cathedral. Two people climbed out: a lady in her forties wearing a bright orange linen blouse, white trousers and sporting dark sunglasses and behind her walked a girl of about fifteen years. Even Katie, with her inexperienced eye, could tell that the young girl with her head down and rounded shoulders was unhappy.

Katie smiled at the pair, as they matched the description she had been given, and beckoned them to her table. The woman gave her name as Judith and the teenager as Laura.

'You don't look old enough to be a reporter,' Judith smiled, quickly looking round at the other customers on the café veranda.

The young reporter explained her position with *The Newburgh Herald* which to her surprise seemed to please Judith. Laura's eyes were still fixed on something imaginary between her two thumbs, twiddling fast. Katie realised that whatever the story was, it involved Laura and she no longer bought into John's theory that the subject was the public loos on Mains Street!

The trio moved indoors to a quiet corner of the café; polite chat followed between Judith and Katie until the coffee and milkshake arrived for the reporter's guests.

'So you have a story that you think might be of interest to our readers? Please tell me about it.' Katie asked, remembering to avoid closed questions.

Judith cleared her throat as she tried to compose herself, took hold of Laura's hand and then she began.

'We're not from this area; we've come down from Wolverhampton. Judith is not my name but this is my daughter; Laura is not her real name either. No one must know who we are or where we're from,' Judith explained to Katie.

Katie's stomach was tightening, she knew she was about to hear something awful but she didn't know what.

'Last Christmas, Laura was invited to a party by one of her classmates. As she was only fourteen at the time, I phoned to check with her friend's mother to make sure there would be adults supervising and that there would be no alcohol or drugs. I was given reassurance and so I allowed Laura to go on the understanding that I would pick her up at nine thirty. Unfortunately, her father was in France on a business trip otherwise he would have collected her. When I arrived at the house Laura was waiting for me; she seemed to have had a good time. But this marked the start of our nightmare,' Judith stopped to clear her throat, nervously adjusting her collar.

'Laura had met an older boy called Wayne at the party, who said he was her friend's cousin. The two chatted and danced a couple of times and somehow Wayne got hold of Laura's mobile number. Laura denies giving it to him but it doesn't matter now anyway. Wayne it turns out was nineteen and had left school but he told Laura he was in his final year at the local sixth form college. He started to text Laura, telling her how 'cool' she was, how grown up she behaved and how much he had enjoyed meeting her. He asked to meet her after school but told Laura not to say anything to anyone, just to keep their friendship a secret. So Laura didn't tell me anything about Wayne; on days she was late in from school, she told me she had been at the after-school computer club, so I didn't suspect anything.'

Katie began to fidget and feel very uncomfortable; she had an idea where this story was going.

'Laura, do you want to tell Katie what happened next?' Judith asked softly, as she turned to look at her daughter.

Laura lifted her head just enough to give Katie a glimpse of her very sad, dark eyes; Katie thought the teenager looked much older than her years. Laura shook her head and lowered her gaze once more.

'Wayne bought Laura lots of presents; I-tune vouchers, jewellery, cosmetics and chocolates but was smart enough to make sure that Laura kept it from me. I blame myself; I was working really hard ...' Judith tailed off, her eyes filling with tears.

Katie reached across and put her hand on the troubled mother's shoulder to comfort her.

'Mum we have to get out of here!' Laura declared as she stood up obviously in distress. 'Can't we go and walk somewhere. You know I hate being in small rooms; people might hear.'

'There's a park just next to the cathedral. Would you like to go there, Laura?' Katie asked considerately, as she tried to reassure the schoolgirl.

The young girl nodded in agreement. The group walked in silence the short distance to the park, settling on the sun-parched grass in a quiet spot by a wall.

To Katie's surprise Laura spoke first.

'It wasn't Mum's fault, it was mine. I should have told Mum what was happening but Wayne told me not to. He said only children told their mothers everything and that as I was a young woman now, I was entitled to my own secrets. I believed him because I thought I loved him. Mum, honestly it wasn't your fault,' Laura said as she reached over and embraced her mother.

Katie sat quietly gazing at her notebook to give the two of them some time. So far she hadn't written down much, only the names of the mother and daughter, but she knew she wouldn't forget any of this story. She could tell this was going to be an emotional journey for all of them by the time it had all been unravelled.

Laura sat up and continued 'Wayne and I started sleeping together. I didn't want to as I knew I was too young. Mum had always said to wait until I was married to the man of my dreams. Wayne said that was so old fashioned, "cool babes enjoyed life to the max". The first time was a Saturday morning, I was supposed to be playing hockey near Oxford so I wasn't expected home until at least four in the afternoon. He told me that his parents were away on business for a few weeks, to somewhere in Eastern Europe; we would go shopping to the mall in the morning and then go to his house for lunch. So I didn't suspect anything when we had the place to ourselves.'

Judith wiped her eyes and smiled at her daughter, nodding to her to continue.

'Wayne made a great lunch but I was a bit nervous when he put wine glasses on the table as I had only ever had a small glass of wine on special occasions, with Mum and Dad's approval. Wayne saw me glancing at the glasses but reminded me I was a "big girl now",' Laura paused again, her gaze locked on the dry ground in front of her. Katie knew the young girl was momentarily back in Wayne's house.

Laura regained her composure and confessed, 'I remember the first glass; I really enjoyed it. Then I started to get giggly, Wayne started to embrace me and before I knew it, we had done it. I was shell-shocked; I really hadn't wanted to go all the way. I wasn't ready; I knew I was too young. Afterwards I looked at the clock; it was three thirty and I had to get home.'

'I knew something had happened that day as you looked upset when you came home Laura; you were very quiet. Both Dad and I noticed but you said you had had a row with Sally, your friend, so we believed you. We were going out that night to Dad's firm's dinner-dance and Granny was looking after you, so I suppose we didn't pay as much attention as we should have,' Judith offered, racked with guilt.

'I texted Wayne the next day and told him that I didn't want to see him again. But he would have none of it. He met me after school and gave me more presents: he bought me a new mobile, a locket and a bracelet. He told me he

loved me and I fell for it; I thought he really loved me,'
Laura explained, as she paused to blow her nose.

She continued, 'We went back to his place again and
again. On one of those visits some of his older cousins came
for the meal as well. I was the only girl which I thought was
a bit weird. There was wine and I smoked my first joint that
day. Wayne took me through to his bedroom as usual but
then his cousins arrived. There were four of them!'

Laura was sobbing now, her mother holding her tightly.

'When Laura came home that night I knew something
awful had gone on. When I confronted her she admitted to
drinking and smoking but nothing else. I knew there was
more but Laura looked exhausted so I let her go to bed and
vowed to get to the bottom of it in the morning,' Judith
continued. 'Unfortunately, Ed, my husband was away on
business to Australia and was not due back for another
few days. He would have demanded an explanation that
night. Maybe then we would have prevented the next stage
of this nightmare.'

'During the evening I texted Wayne and said I was never
going to see him again and if he came near me I was going
to the police. He sent back a photograph of me. It was
awful! One of his cousins must have taken it. He told me
that if I didn't meet him at ten that night he would send
the picture all round my friends and to my parents. I didn't
want my parents to be so hurt and disgusted with me so
I sneaked out of my bedroom window and met him. He
kissed me then he bundled me into the back of a posh
car, one a bit like Dad's silver one. In the back seat was
his cousin, the one with the black beard, he just leered at
me and grabbed me by the hair to pull me towards him.
Wayne jumped in beside me ... I was trapped.'

Chapter 8

The Hunt

By the end of week four, in his new role as village doctor, Tim was beginning to relax. He felt he had coped well with everything that had come his way: from sick kids, to ante-natal checks, to fractured limbs. All in all he was quite pleased with himself. It was Friday, almost the weekend; Miguel announced they were going to have a celebration on the Saturday night to mark the end of their first six months in Nueva Casa. Tim and Ronaldo were invited to join Miguel and the hunters on their expedition to track down something special for the occasion.

The next morning, just before first light, the hunters were off to an area of the jungle Tim hadn't visited since his arrival, but well away from the mining area. They were looking for peccary, small pig-like creatures that the vil-lagers hunted. Tim was relieved they weren't looking for monkeys as he had promised himself he wouldn't eat these for fear of catching an exotic viral illness. He knew from the little tropical medicine he had studied that it was possible to catch some real nasties from bushmeat but he hoped these pig-like creatures would be safer … already he was fed up with chicken and rice!

The womenfolk and children were very excited. The first few months in the new village had been hard work. The men folk had laboured daily to give every family a roof over their heads. Ground was cleared to plant the first crop of yuca, the potato like vegetable that was the staple diet. The men felled trees to make rafts which were anchored to the bank so the ladies could go down to the river to wash themselves and their clothes. To build a new school was one of headteacher Miguel's first priorities; he wanted to be able to teach right through the rainy season so a new construction was required. His wife Maria shared the teaching with him as his headman duties kept him busy.

Tim enjoyed the one hour canoe trip, powered initially by the small pecky-pecky engine. Just after they turned up a tributary of the Rio Waldoo, the hunters cut the engines; they didn't want to startle their prey so they had to paddle hard for another half an hour. The hunters were super fit and Tim had difficulty keeping pace so he diverted his thoughts away from his aching limbs by listening to the bird calls and the monkey screeches. He was thrilled to see, along the opposite bank, scarlet macaws flying in formation like an aerial display team. Grey dolphins broke the surface in the middle of the river and then dived gracefully beneath the surface. Their canoe hugged the right riverbank as they continued upstream but as they rounded a bend in the river a commotion in the canopy caught their attention. There was a group of spider monkeys chasing each other through trees, startling the parrots that then flew across the river to the safety of the other bank.

Low water meant that at times they had to avoid the mudflats that reached into the river from the shore. Tim held his breath as he saw two huge camen basking on one such mudflat; he wasn't the only one to be afraid. Miguel stopped paddling and reached to the floor of the canoe for his machete, placing it securely in his belt ... just in case the reptiles made a dash for the canoe as it passed; the creatures were certainly capable of up-ending the little vessel and leaving them all swimming for their lives. The team were heading for a place known to Cesar, the oldest of the hunters; he was a man in his forties who had lived in this area for many years, but had only recently joined the community of Nueva Casa, bringing with him his wife and five children.

At a small inlet they pulled the canoe onto the bank, and secured it well. Stealthily the six men headed off along the track following the small stream. Tim found the going tough; he was sweating, breathing hard and he thought his heart was going to burst out of his chest as he jogged behind the others. He knew he should have made a greater effort to keep himself fit while he was working in London. Tim used to ask his patients: why did they eat so much, drink so much alcohol, and not take enough exercise? He was a bit more humble now, when he realised that he too had failed to keep himself fit, he too had eaten too much and was carrying extra kilos ... and now he was paying the price! Things had to change in his life and he knew it.

Miguel was the first to see Tim was lagging behind so called a rest, receiving some strange looks from the real hunters. Fortunately there was only another half mile to go and the track was good. Refreshed by some water the group headed off again. Ten minutes further up the track Cesar spoke with Miguel and then they divided the group into two.

Cesar and two of the village men followed a track to the right leading further into the forest while Tim and Ronaldo followed Miguel off to the left, a route which led up a steep slope and to a rocky outcrop. Miguel signalled to the lads to be quiet as they crept forward on their bellies to peer down to the stream. About fifty metres below them was a quiet pool with a gravel area in front of a grassy bank. The jungle undergrowth reached to within about three metres of the river, just to the left of the pool. Ronaldo nudged Tim and pointed to these bushes; there hiding, blow pipe armed and ready, was Cesar. But where were the other two? Tim wondered.

As if he had read Tim's thoughts Ronaldo pointed to a thicket just to the right of the pool, the two younger men were crouched ready for action too.

'How long will we have to wait?' Tim whispered to Miguel.

'How long is a piece of fishing line? You gringos don't have much patience do you?' he teased. 'We may be here an hour, maybe two, but most animals come to drink early before they settle down for the day. Cesar said that he has found peccary at this pool several times before, so here's hoping, otherwise we'll have to have chicken for our celebration. Surely we can do better than that!'

Tim was just recovering from his 'yomp' through the jungle when three peccaries trotted innocently onto the gravel. They sniffed the air and when satisfied no danger lurked they continued to the water. Cesar and the hunters struck in an instant, their darts hitting two of the animals but the third escaped. The noise that followed from the screeching of the wild boar like creatures was both deafening and disturbing to Tim. He was a city boy and didn't like the idea of killing animals for food; he was happy to admit to being one of the many meat-eaters in the modern world who liked to fill his supermarket trolley with meat products, without having to think where they had come from. However, he also realised that these animals of the forest were an essential food source for the villagers and their families, but at that moment he could see the attraction of being a vegetarian!

The injured peccaries ran off into the jungle with the hunters in hot pursuit, a chase the men were accustomed to. The animals would run until the poison on the dart had infiltrated their nervous system, paralysing them and bringing them down.

'All we have to do now is go down to the pool and wait for the others to return with the game. Come on,' Miguel said as he clambered over the rocks.

Sure enough, about half an hour later, Cesar and the other hunters appeared triumphantly with two lifeless peccary tied onto poles, ready for the journey back to the village.

The evening was very special for the Nueva Casa family. They danced, sang and ate until very late. Tim managed to eat some of the roasted peccary with a bit of encouragement from his friends who had come to accept that the young doctor would never be a hunter unless his life depended on it. Some of the local alcoholic drink, masato, was handed round the adults and after a few hours of celebration the men folk were very cheerful and joined in the dancing with a new ferocity and enthusiasm. Tim declined the beverage as he was all too aware of how the brew was made. The much chewing and spitting of yuca roots into vats by the womenfolk had put him off; the thought of someone's broken tooth in his cup was just too much for him!

Tim slipped away from the revellers at about midnight, back to his hut. He had enjoyed himself but was quite exhausted from the hunt and the heat had got to him more than usual. Since he had sweated excessively most of the day, and to prevent him waking with cramp in the night, he took some salt supplements before he tumbled into his hammock and fell fast asleep.

'Is that you Ronaldo?' Tim asked as he peered into the darkness to see who was standing beside his hammock. He could just make out the shape of a man on the other side of the mosquito net.

Suddenly a flashlight blinded him! Something, cold and hard was forced against his left temple. He knew in an instant he was in mortal danger, but from whom?

'Not a word gringo! Move one muscle or even twitch and I'll pull this trigger!' the unknown figure grunted, in a Spanish accent Tim knew was not local.

The man ripped down the net and pulled his victim to the floor. Tim was made to lie face down with arms outstretched while handcuffs were put on him, then he was yanked to his feet. By now Tim realised there were at least four men in his hut. He worried about Ronaldo and hoped he wouldn't return for a while.

'Our boss needs a doctor and you're the only one in town! Where do you keep your gringo medicines?' the man with the gun demanded.

Before Tim had time to answer the gunman brought the pistol across Tim's face knocking him to the floor.

'Too slow Doc. I expect an answer straightaway. Just so you understand!'

'In the rucksack under the table,' Tim answered, wiping the blood from his face as best he could with cuffed hands.

The gunman gesticulated to one of the others who picked up the load. His captors helped him to put on his boots and then, at Tim's request they collected his stethoscope and two medical books before he was bundled out of the back of the hut into the jungle. Still dazed from the blow to his head, he was taken, half carried, on a five minute forced march to a waiting fast boat. He was thrown into the bottom of the vessel and told not to move if he wanted to live. The rib sped off down the Rio Waldoo and turned north up the Rio Tigre. After half an hour Tim knew that they were not stopping in Intuto but heading towards Ecuador. This had to be one of the criminal drug gangs and he had just been kidnapped!

Chapter 9

Skirmish

The fast boat continued at great speed up the Rio Tigre. Tim remained curled up on the floor of the boat; every time he tried to make himself comfortable he was kicked by one of the guards. The young medic tried to work out if they were still racing up the main river or if they had turned off up a tributary but it was impossible for him to tell.

'Don't kick him so hard you idiot,' the group leader shouted at Tim's assailant. 'The boss wants him alive and fit to look after his lady, remember! If you smash him up, the boss ain't going to be pleased with you.'

'Sorry boss. But you know I don't like gringos, doctor or not,' the other answered, coldly.

Hearing this conversation gave Tim at least some reassurance that, for now, he was safe; they had some use for him.

'Sit him up and give him some water,' the gang leader barked.

Tim was manhandled into a sitting position and given a drink. The rough tugging of the thug resulted in half the water running down Tim's chin onto his T-shirt.

'Where're you from boy?' the leader asked gruffly, chewing on some leaves, probably from the coca plant.

'London,' Tim replied softly, as he tried to wipe the blood off his cheek with his arm.

'Where's that? Are you a Yank?'

'No, I'm from Britain,' Tim clarified, hoping this might just help his cause a little.

'You're a long way from home. What' you doing here?' the leader continued.

'Helping my friend, the chief of Nueva Casa. They have no doctor in Intuto so he asked me to come for a few months.'

'How do you know the chief? You' been here before?'

Before Tim could answer, a spotlight lit up the vessel from a craft sitting by the bank. The bandits pulled back the throttle of their fast boat lifting the nose high out of the water and forcing Tim right back against the stern of the boat. One of the gang fell back landing beside the captive.

'Army patrol! Let's get out of here,' the leader screamed to his men.

Tim was pulled down to the floor of the boat and on this occasion he was more than happy to curl up there while bullets whizzed above him. The boat twisted and turned violently for the next few minutes. The gang were returning fire but still the patrol boat pursued them.

'Get the light! Shoot out the lights,' the leader ordered frantically.

One of the gang collapsed in the bottom beside Tim, blood pouring from his abdomen. Tim instinctively found himself trying to help him but couldn't because of his handcuffs. One of the others quickly saw the problem and released Tim to attend to his new 'patient'. Bullets still strafed the boat as it continued to zigzag up river.

Suddenly everything was in darkness; the kidnappers had managed to shoot out the searchlight. The gang let out a cheer as they knew escape was almost certain now. It was a cloudy night so it should be easy for them to slip up a tributary and lie low for a couple of hours before heading on their way.

Tim tried his best to stop the bleeding from the bandit's gut. The wounded fighter was about the same age as Tim, much stockier and more muscular but this didn't matter now; he was haemorrhaging fast. Tim couldn't see the blood in the darkness but he could feel the warm life-giving fluid on his patient's soaked clothes. The doctor couldn't find a pulse at the boy's wrist or his elbow so he knew the bandit was losing blood rapidly and in big trouble. Tim pulled off his T-shirt, folded it into a pad, and tied it tight with his belt round the man's waist, but there was nothing else he could do for him. To survive this man needed urgent surgery and he wasn't going to get that any time soon.

The wounded man reached up and pulled Tim close.

'Why you do that for me? Thank you,' he mumbled in Spanish and with that he slipped into unconsciousness.

For the next ten minutes or so, the fast boat continued upstream as quickly as possible before it veered sharply to the right into a tributary of the Tigre. After a further fifty metres the engines were cut and the small craft allowed to drift back downstream towards the Tigre. The helmsman cleverly tucked the vessel behind a clump of trees that had slipped into the river when the bank was undermined by the flood waters. Tim realised these guys knew this part of the jungle like the back of their hands; they couldn't have found this hideaway without previous knowledge.

Anxious minutes followed as the gang sat in silence, watching and listening for the army boat. Tim knew that if the military found them, there would be a huge fight and probably little chance of escape. Yet again he would find himself on the wrong side of the Peruvian authorities, just as he had when he was mistaken for a street child in Iquitos all those years ago. He still couldn't believe how he and Katie had survived the air crash in the jungle but then had almost been killed by the Peruvian police. Now he was about to be mistaken for a drug terrorist. If he survived this then maybe, he should just stay away from Peru, he thought.

They could hear the army patrol boat as it came up the Tigre. The soldiers had managed to rig up another light and were searching the river. The light was swung round to the right revealing the tributary; the patrol boat stopped and engines were cut while the lookout peered up the smaller river. The soldiers were listening for any engine noise, any clue that would indicate which way the terrorists had gone. The kidnappers were tense, hands on weapons. Tim's patient started to moan and writhe about in pain; the young medic quickly leaned over the victim to lessen the noise. Tense minutes passed. Tim was confused: why was he protecting his kidnappers? he asked himself. But he knew it would be certain death if they were found because these guys would never surrender; they would fight to the end!

The splutter of the patrol boat engine starting and then the sound disappearing up river was a huge relief to Tim and his captors. No one moved for about five minutes other than the injured man who continued to struggle for breath in the bottom of the boat. Then suddenly he stopped, the man was completely still, Tim couldn't hear his laboured breathing anymore. The young doctor searched about for a pulse but could feel none. He bent over the young man again, this time to listen for signs of life. There were none.

Tim could feel the eyes of the other kidnappers pierce his back as they waited for a response from him.

'He's dead', Tim reported calmly, praying that no one would blame him for not being able to save the fighter.

'I didn't think he would make it,' the leader grunted. 'The rounds the army use destroy a man. No one recovers from a shot in the gut.'

The rest of the fighters crossed themselves as a mark of respect for the dead man, a tradition their mothers had probably taught them as children. But these were not emotional comrades; they were hardened fighters, seasoned by years of brutal criminal activity. Tim wondered how men ended up associated with such gangs. Was it poverty? Was it bravado? Something real men had to do in the Columbian slums, from which they were probably recruited, to gain street 'cred', he concluded.

After a couple of minutes the leader of the gang declared, 'We'll have to sit it out until that patrol boat heads back down to Intuto; we don't want to "bang" into them again. Let's hope we got one of them because they'll want to get him back to their medic.'

'Hey gringo! I saw what you did; you tried to save him. He was the guy who was kicking you. Why did you help him?' one of the fighters asked Tim.

'I'm a Christian, we help our enemies,' Tim answered softly.

'He's a man of God, as well as a doctor,' the leader laughed, shaking his head in disbelief.

'Well you'd better get praying boy because our boss is no man of God,' the terrorist continued, laughing loudly much to the hilarity of the rest of the gang.

'Where are you taking me? What do you want from me?

Tim asked his captors now that they seemed a little more relaxed with him.

'Our boss has a little camp in the jungle where we do a bit of mining work. The boss's lady is pregnant; he wants a doctor to look after her.

'Why? Nearly all of the girls give birth round here without anyone other than older women of their community. Is there a problem?' Tim enquired, somewhat puzzled.

'His lady lost the last one at birth. The boss promised her a doctor the next time and he's a man of his word,' the leader, Eduardo, smirked.

'Why doesn't she go to the hospital in Iquitos?' Tim asked innocently.

The men sneered at his suggestion.

Eduardo continued, 'Neither of them can be seen in Iquitos. If they get caught they're looking at a long time in prison … twenty years maybe!'

'Mmm, not good. How long will it be until we reach the camp?' Tim asked to try to get some bearings.

'If I tell you I'll have to shoot you! And I'm a man of my word too! Enough questions from you, God man,' Eduardo said waving his pistol in Tim's direction.

The men sat in silence for over forty minutes. Tim thought the noise of the jungle seemed louder than usual, possibly because he like the others was straining to hear any distant rumbles of an engine. The clouds had lifted and the moon was now high in the sky; if the army did find them there would be nowhere to hide now.

One of the kidnapers anxiously watched the trees as some of the branches hung over the vessel; Tim shared his concern. An anaconda could easily slip down and join them in the boat or one of the smaller, very poisonous, green backs could just drop onto the deck and take a bite out of any of them. A nip from this snake would be fatal in less than an hour. For a moment Tim was glad his captors had large knives tucked into their belts. The kidnappers, who were seasoned jungle men, became more and more disgruntled as they were driven mad by the mosquitoes! The combination of water, heat and sweaty bodies attracted the blood suckers in their droves.

'How much longer are we gonna sit here boss?' one of the fighters asked Eduardo, as he slapped another biting bug from his arm.

'Who knows? But we can't move until the patrol boat heads back down to Intuto,' came the reply in a tone that said 'don't ask again'.

Tim could see the bats flying around in the moonlight. He didn't like bats; out here many of them were infected with the rabies virus, so a bite could easily give the victim the terrifying hydrophobic disease. He was glad he had had his rabies jabs before he left home; he knew there was no cure for this horrible infection so he wasn't going to take any chances. Only a few years ago he had heard of a terrible outbreak in the Brazilian jungle which had killed several Indians.

Suddenly something moved in the shallow water by the bank, then another movement. Nervous, one of the kidnappers shone his torch towards the sound; three pairs of eyes reflected back at him.

'Camen!' he cried. 'At least three of them and they're huge.'

'Put that light out you idiot! Do you want the army to find us?' Eduardo said as he thumped the other on the back. 'Listen do you hear that? They're coming back.'

'About time, I'm getting eaten alive,' said another fighter, shifting restlessly in the bow.

Fortunately for all, the army boat sped past and headed back to base in Intuto. Once no engine sound could be heard the kidnappers fired up their fast boat and then slipped out from their hiding place into the Tigre once more. Tim was bundled onto the floor again which meant he had to share the cramped space with the corpse. The journey seemed to go on and on; on several occasions Tim was sure they turned off the Tigre up smaller rivers but in the darkness he just couldn't tell.

The cutting of the engines signalled to Tim that they were near their destination; mercifully they had not encountered any more of the military. Tim reckoned it must have been around three in the morning.

His captors marched him across the village to a building with bars on the window and a guard at the door. In the moonlight Tim could see he had arrived at quite a large community, much bigger than Nueva Casa. There was much noise and hilarity coming from a saloon on the other side of the square; several drunks staggering about with girls on their arms. Eduardo kicked the sleeping guard into action and the prison was unlocked. Tim was thrown onto the floor of the gloomy shack and the door locked firmly behind him.

'Sleep tight, God man,' Eduardo jeered, as he headed off to the saloon with the rest of the fighters.

Tim lay on the mud floor for a few minutes and tried to work out if all this was real or just a dream. His face was still hurting, a tooth on his lower jaw was lose and his ribs ached from one of the many kicks he had received; this was no dream, this was fast becoming a nightmare.

'Hey do you speak English?' a weak voice with an American accent spoke from the corner, shattering the silence.

'Yes. Who're you?' Tim replied, as he peered into the darkness towards the voice.

'The name's Rick. I'm an American.'

'What are you doing here? How long have you been here?' Tim asked, anxiously looking for answers.

'I was kidnapped from an oilfield that I reckon is about six hours by fast boat from here. I was turned in for the night, in my hut, when a bunch of guys armed to the teeth burst in, tied me up and bundled me into a boat and brought me here,' Rick explained.

'How long ago was that? Why did they kidnap you? Who are they?' Tim continued, desperately trying to make sense of the situation.

'Hey, slow down we've plenty of time to talk. About two weeks ago. They're a terrorist group similar to The Shining Path. They've a cocaine factory here and from what I've heard they've reopened an old gold mine. They've asked for a million dollars for me to be paid by the end of the month; ten days from now!' Rick replied unfolding more of his story.

'Or?'

'I'll be a goner,' Rick said, with a tremble in his voice.

'Surely not! Who's to pay the ransom? Why are you so important to them?' Tim asked seeking further information.

'The US government. I'm a professor of geology, seconded to the Peruvians. Somebody must have told these thugs that I was working in the Loreto region; I'm a prize catch for these guys.'

'I've heard of Shining Path; they were a terrorist organisation in the eighties. I thought they were all in jail?' Tim muttered, incredulously.

'The original group are securely locked up and the leaders are unlikely to ever be set free, after everything they did. This lot call themselves The Black Vultures and they've modelled themselves on "The Path" but it's not known if they have any direct links to the remnants of that particular nasty bunch. They certainly know how to terrorise people just like "The Path" did; in reality they are just another criminal gang.'

'Sounds like an apt name for them. They're thugs alright!' Tim said holding his ribs as each breath was painful.

'Hey, have they broken your ribs?' the American asked. 'There rough that's for sure; my face feels a bit of a mess but there's no mirror, which is probably good.'

'I think I'm just bruised. I can't see you properly in this light. Tell me what you know about this place,' Tim requested.

'I've kept watch through the bars since I arrived, mainly to see if there was any possibility of escape. It looks to me as if the workforce here is made up of villagers trafficked from all parts of Amazonia, probably around a hundred of them. The boy who brings my food is only about ten years old; he has some Spanish so I have learnt a fair bit from him. There's at least fifty heavily armed, violent thugs as well, just to make sure everybody works. Over in the cantina there must be thirty or maybe more women; some of them just young teens, also trafficked here to amuse the fighters.'

'It's a big operation then.'

'What about you? What do they want with you?' Rick asked of his new cellmate.

'I'm a doctor. The leader of this outfit's lady is about to give birth. She lost the first one so the boss promised her a doctor for the next. I'm the only one for seventy miles. So they asked me along with a little help from a few rifles.'

'I wouldn't like to be in your shoes; I hope you are good at what you do. If the Baron loses his lady ... You haven't met the Baron yet, have you?' Rick said in frightening tones.

Chapter 10

Time to Find Out More

Laura continued her story, ringing her hands as she recalled the terrible car journey and the events that followed, 'For about half an hour or more, Wayne and his cousin kept a tight hold of me in the back of the car. They forced my head onto my lap so I couldn't see where they were taking me. I was terrified and could hardly breathe; I thought I was going to pass out. I remember that when we arrived in the street it was a horrible wet night; I was forced out of the car and up a staircase into a cold flat that stunk of sweat and dirty, damp clothes. The place was poorly lit and dingy; Wayne threw me into the bedroom and locked the door. I lay on the floor and sobbed.'

Katie tried to imagine the 'hell' the young woman sitting next to her had gone through; a shiver went down her spine as she thought of the teenager's fear as she entered the flat, not sure if she was going to live or die. The reporter admired Laura's courage as she continued to share her ordeal.

'I must have lain there for hours, too frightened to move. I could hear Wayne and his cousins talking about me, I doubt they really were relatives at all. They were discussing what they were going to do with me. I still couldn't believe that Wayne was bad, he had been so nice to me but I knew from experience how cruel his cousins could be.'

Laura started to cry into her hankie, her mother comforting her gently.

'I'll tell you the rest,' Judith said, taking a big deep breath and fighting for composure.

'Laura was abused by Wayne and his friends for the next two weeks. Sometimes strangers came and Laura is convinced that Wayne was paid money for each man that came into her room. She was fed badly but when she complained and said she wanted to go home Wayne slapped her. He threatened that if she tried to escape he would pick up her little sister; Polly is only twelve.'

Katie looked at Judith and thought of her own mother, and then understood more clearly the very dark place this family had found themselves. She knew it wasn't just Laura who was the victim in this disaster.

'The evening Laura disappeared I phoned the police and reported her missing. They asked if she had a boyfriend and by that time I had found out about Wayne from Sally, who seemed to be the only friend who knew anything about him. Once the police heard that Laura had a boyfriend they concluded she had run away with him and they were not at all convinced by my story that she had been kidnapped.'

Judith blew her nose and then continued.

'After two weeks Laura was bundled into a car again and moved to another place, this time a house. There she met a young woman who was a few years older than her called Christina; she was going through the same ordeal as Laura. Both girls were imprisoned in the building and had to entertain men every night; they endured beatings if the customer was not satisfied by their behaviour. The girls daren't try to escape as they were continually warned that their younger siblings would suffer the same fate if they attempted to leave the house. In effect they were controlled by these wicked people, treated like animals; it was sexual slavery.'

Judith wrung her hands as she paused for a moment. Laura sat with her head bowed, her fingers playing with the daisies in the grass and then suddenly, every now and again, she would pull off the head of a flower. Katie could see that the young girl was severely traumatised.

Laura's mother continued with the story.

'This went on for about another three weeks. The police were making a few enquires but my husband and I knew the detectives had decided that Laura had gone off with her boyfriend or just run away. One police sergeant was very unhelpful when he informed us that he had seen this sort of thing many times before!'

For the first time Katie could see anger in Judith's face; she understood why the mother felt so frustrated with the police.

'You must've been so angry that no one believed your story that Laura had been kidnapped,' Katie commented, sympathetically.

Judith nodded in agreement before carrying on.

'One morning Laura and Christina had a stroke of luck. Wayne and the men who stayed in the house had all gone out leaving a young man on his own to look after them. Before the men left, the girls were locked in their room as usual. That morning the girls decided to make their escape. They had stolen some matches from the kitchen and some bits of newspaper. They lit the paper in a metal waste bin and positioned it by the door; they waited until there was a good bit of smoke and then they shouted … fire, fire! The young man was fooled; he came running and unlocked the door. The girls had made a trip wire from some electric cable … it worked a treat! The youth fell flat on his face inside the room; the girls didn't miss their chance.'

Laura had recovered her poise and with a smile continued the story.

'We quickly shut the door and locked it; we ran through to the kitchen and out the back of the house and then off! We had no idea where we were, but we didn't care, we were free. After walking for about ten minutes we came to a hospital; we went into the Accident and Emergency Department. I pretended I had twisted my ankle so I could speak to a doctor and then tell them what had happened to us. I was under sixteen so I knew they would have to help us.'

'That was a really clever thing to do Laura', Katie commented. 'I suppose you didn't want to walk the streets for too long in case Wayne and his friends came back and found out you were missing.'

'Yes, I think they would have killed us!' Laura replied. 'In fact I know they would have murdered us and dumped us in a wood somewhere.'

'The next thing we knew was when the police arrived at the door with Laura,' Judith continued. 'Ed and I couldn't believe it; we were overjoyed to see our lovely daughter back.'

'This time Laura told us everything. But she had no idea where she had been held, she didn't know where Wayne lived. The police carried out some investigations but couldn't make any arrests,' Judith reported, disgusted that no one had been held accountable for her daughter's grooming and abuse.

'The next morning, there was a big brown envelop pushed through the door, addressed to Laura. Inside there were horrible photographs of her and a threatening letter. The garage door had all sorts of obscenities daubed on it. Ed and I realised then we had to get Laura and the rest of the family away from our home to a safe place so we sent her and her sister to friends in Wales,' Judith revealed, looking a bit happier now.

'How long ago was all this?' Katie asked trying to get the story into some sort of timescale.

'Laura returned to us at the end of May,' Judith answered, smiling at her daughter.

'Have the police arrested anyone?' Katie questioned, sure that three months later, someone would be behind bars.

'No. All the enquiries so far have led nowhere. They think that Wayne and his "cousins" are probably out of the country, lying low somewhere in Eastern Europe. He wasn't a real cousin of Laura's friend either, it was all lies.

We were so angry by the way the local police handled the case that we went to The Police Complaints Commission. Eventually we received an apology from the Chief Constable and an admission that something similar had happened in London, but again no one was arrested,' Judith replied.

'What happened to Christina?' Katie asked, suddenly remembering the other young victim.

'She was from Moldova. She was tricked into thinking she was going to work as nanny for a professional family in Paris. She met her trafficker in a café in her local town but she was kidnapped as she waited for the bus to take her back to her village. The poor girl was smuggled into the UK six months ago. Happily she has been reunited with her mother,' Laura explained, allowing herself a little smile.

'So there you have the story, Katie,' Judith declared. 'We want you to publish it so that every parent knows of the dangers out there for their children. We want school teachers and youth workers to be able to recognise the signs of grooming. There are predators out there who see young girls as a commodity; we want everyone to know this sexual exploitation is going on in our country.'

Judith was quite animated at this point, determined that this awful nightmare that had fallen on her family should not happen to others.

'What now for Laura?' Katie asked gently, thinking that a long process of counselling and psychological help would be required.

'We are moving to another country, starting a new life; fortunately we can afford to do this but others can't. Laura has been through a terrible ordeal: she needs time to recover, time to heal all those psychological scars. We are leaving tomorrow, to a new beginning,' Judith revealed, obviously now much more relaxed.

'My Mum and Dad have been terrific ... they love me so much. I just wish I had told them about Wayne right at the beginning, I might have spared them all this pain. It was my idea to go to the papers as I don't want any other girl to go through what I've been through. Katie, please make sure this is published,' Laura pleaded grasping Katie's hands.

'We have to go now; we still have a lot of packing to do. Katie, please don't try and identify us, for Laura's sake. Thank you for listening,' Judith said, as she stood up and hugged the young reporter.

'Thanks Katie. Please make sure this is published,' Laura said, as she too embraced the young journalist.

———

Katie watched as Judith's car disappeared under the fly-over en route to the motorway. Would she ever see them again? she wondered. Shocked to the core, after hearing of Laura's terrible nightmare, the student journalist recognised that it was now up to her to let the world know all about it.

Not sure what to do first, Katie glanced at her watch, four forty-five, no point in travelling back to the office now, she thought. The student decided to walk along the river past the cathedral; it was a beautiful evening and she had a lot on her mind. The bells were ringing out inviting worshippers to come in for evensong. As she walked round to the front of the cathedral she felt a sudden desire to go into the church. Katie attended church at university; she played in the Praise Band, but in truth she had felt confused about her faith recently, she had so many unanswered questions, so many doubts. This night, though, she had a strong urge to take timeout with God.

Cathedrals weren't really Katie's thing she preferred a smaller church, where she knew most of the congregation – something less grand. As she walked down the central aisle she could hear the choir singing at the front and could see the worshippers gathered near the altar. Strangely, Katie wanted none of that so she stepped into the left and slid along to the end of the row, beside a huge stone column. Katie slumped in the chair and bent over as if to pray, but Laura's story was whizzing around in her mind so much that she couldn't pray. The young reporter was deeply troubled by what she had heard that afternoon.

She had so many questions in her head. Why would someone deliberately target such a nice, well brought up kid? Katie became annoyed with herself as she realised that was a ridiculous point of view. The question should be 'Why would anyone target any child, from any back-ground, and force them to have sex with men?' The answer hit her like a sledge hammer … money! If one guy was doing it for money, and he was prepared to spend months building a relationship with Laura then there must be other men, out there, right now, 'grooming' other young naïve girls. Katie felt sick! Then the tears came; Katie couldn't contain her emotions any more, the sheer wickedness of what she had heard that afternoon was too much for her.

As she was drying her eyes the music stopped and the preacher's voice boomed around the magnificent building. His bible text for the evening was 'don't let evil conquer you but conquer evil with good.'

Katie pricked up her ears as the preacher repeated the verse. He then went on to say 'in a world where there is so much evil …' The young woman heard no more, her head was in her hands as she repeated the verse over and over to herself. Then she started to pray. 'I know it's no accident I'm hearing this verse just now. I know You want me to do something about Laura and others like her, please give wisdom to my young mind so I can do my best to put a stop to this evil.' After her prayer Katie felt a great peace.

She knew she had a job to do and no matter what, she was going to do her part.

She left the cathedral refreshed and with a spring in her step. After supper she knew it was going to be a long night; she planned to search the internet for news reports from different parts of the UK and around the world to try and find out just how big a problem 'grooming' was. If she hoped to persuade her editor to act, she knew she had to do the homework first.

———◈———

After supper, around eight o'clock, Katie sat down at her computer and typed 'sexual exploitation' into the search engine. She couldn't believe the number of pages that came up, and within seconds. As she expected, the young reporter found press reports from Far Eastern countries following high profile prosecutions. She had heard of these before, some were British citizens who had travelled to places such as Cambodia and Vietnam intent on abusing children. At least some of those countries were cracking down on such activities but she had a hunch that most men were never caught or bribed their way out of trouble.

Katie knew that street children in Peru were at risk from sexual exploitation too. Kids that had been helped by the children's charity that her family had set up would tell gruelling stories of sexual abuse; many of these youngsters were badly disturbed. Rescued boys and girls would talk to their carers about being abused by Western men for a few coins, enough to buy some food. She knew that these were stark choices for children: abuse or starvation.

Thinking about the street boys of Iquitos reminded Katie

of Andres. He was one of the young boys who had saved her and Tim from the police and hidden them with the gang in the sewer. Andres knew that Katie was hungry so he stole some chocolate from a market stall, but the boy was set upon by a security guard who beat him so badly that he died, a few hours later, in the sewer. Katie could feel her eyes moisten as she thought of Andres' kindness towards her and yet it had cost him his life. If only the gang leader Rico had been found, she thought, we could have helped him come off the streets; she wondered if he was still alive. Katie began to wish she was in Peru with Tim; she would have loved to go with him to Miguel's village, she could have helped in the school for the summer. Tim will be having a great time, she decided, a real modern day Dr Livingstone.

A video clip caught her eye with the picture of a blue-eyed, blonde-haired girl in her young teens; it was entitled 'He said he loved me.' With a deep breath Katie hit the play button; the young girl had an American accent, she was from Florida. The young woman told a story so like Laura's that it sent a shiver down Katie's spine. This youngster, who in the film was using the false name of Chloe, had at the age of thirteen met a boy, Kurt, who said he was sixteen and from another school. This boy told Chloe how beautiful she was, gave her gifts, and told her not to tell her parents, just as in the case of Laura. This went on for six months, Chloe thought she was deeply in love and that Kurt loved her as well. A similar progression occurred: drink followed by sleeping together, the other boys, the awful photographs, the threats and finally the trafficking out of her home area to big cities where she was sold for sex. Her parents were both professional people who thought their daughter was being a stroppy teenager with mood swings and tantrums. When she failed to come home one night they were beside themselves with anxiety; they contacted the police but when the officers heard there was a boyfriend, just as in the case of Laura, they lost interest and said that Chloe was a runaway! Chloe by this time was a virtual prisoner, held with two other American girls in Chicago. They were told that if they tried to escape their parents would receive the compromising photographs and learn that they were now prostitutes. By pure chance the apartment where they were being held was above a store which had a small explosion after a gas leak. The men guarding them ran off leaving the girls locked in the bedroom. They were rescued by firemen who heard their cries for help as they evacuated the building. The girls were reunited with their parents in safe houses and supported by a new government agency dealing with internal trafficking in the USA.

Katie began to realise that if this sort of thing was happening in America then chances are it was going on in the UK. Running her eye down the next page of the internet search, she noticed a newspaper based in Newcastle had reported on a court case where three men in their forties were accused of grooming young girls from Teesside. Katie read the report and again found disturbing similarities to both Laura and Chloe's story. She continued hunting round the web until she found the outcome of the trial. The men were acquitted through lack of evidence! Katie wondered if the girls were so intimidated that they refused to testify against their abusers.

By two in the morning, Katie had discovered other reports of suspected cases of teenagers being taken from one city to another and used in the sex industry but no prosecutions. If cases did get to court, they invariably collapsed through lack of firm evidence.

The young reporter tried a different tack. Katie had always associated the term 'trafficking' with illegal drugs and the movement of drugs between countries yet she noted the word was being used in several of the reports she had read. Time to put 'trafficking' into the search engine she decided. Again many articles appeared, some dealt with the abduction and movement of young women and girls from Eastern European countries; these victims were forced to move to Western Europe, Britain and America and work in the sex industry. Others were accounts of victims trafficked by gang masters to work in dangerous mines or cotton fields in different parts of the world.

Katie began to see words like slavery in many of these articles. She knew of the African slaves of the eighteenth century and she was well aware of the terrific accomplishment of William Wilberforce the great abolitionist who succeeded, just before he died, in making slavery illegal around the British Empire.

The student was so tired she couldn't focus any more; time for bed.

Chapter 11

To Do or Die

The guard fumbled with the padlocks on the door and the clank of his keys wakened Tim. With his sore ribs Tim had found sleep difficult lying on the mud floor; he just couldn't get comfortable on the hard uneven surface. His mind was working overtime too, as he had tried to absorb everything that had been thrown at him that awful night, but he must have dozed off. The young doctor had to fight off complete despair by thinking of all the positives. He decided to thank God that: he had survived the attack by the army; the terrorists had to look after him, at least for now, because they wanted his skills; and for his new companion who could give him some knowledge of the camp. Every time he felt down he promised himself he would focus on the plus points; he knew it would be the only way to survive this ordeal.

Through bleary tired eyes, Tim could see the sun streaming in through the bars on the windows. Rick was rousing too and for the first time Tim was able to see his cellmate. The guard kicked Tim in the leg to get him up. Two men were waiting for him outside, each armed with submachine guns; they signalled to him to walk across the grassy area to a large lodge on the other side of the village. It seemed an extremely bright sunny morning to Tim, so it took him a few minutes to adjust his eyes. To his left was the river where he could just make out the fast boat tied among several similar craft. To his right the forest had been cleared and he could see men hard at work. There were armed men everywhere, some on sentry duty just watching the workforce, others walking up and down the riverbank. The saloon was quiet now but several young girls proceeded from the building, heading down to the river to wash. Tim saw how young some of them were but he couldn't understand why there were so many young women in such a remote place.

The naïve captive was ushered into the building. It was well equipped with proper seating, tables and chairs. There was a kitchen area with a sink and a fridge powered by a generator that Tim could hear rumbling out the back. Tim glimpsed, through an open door at the back of the building, a bedroom with a double bed and proper linen, something he didn't expect to see in the jungle. Out of the room came a middle-aged man, who was obviously the 'Baron' followed by a very pregnant young woman. The man had jet black hair, combed straight back, a deep red cravat around his neck and white shirt. His misshapen nose told Tim he had been in a few scrapes and that he was a tough character.

'You must be the doctor,' the Baron said gruffly. 'I hope my boys have treated you gently. Has anyone told you why we brought you here?'

'Yes, you need a doctor,' Tim replied softly.

'Raquel, my woman, is due to have her baby. She lost the last one. You are going to make sure she doesn't lose this one,' the Baron pronounced, as he came over to Tim and glared into his eyes.

Tim saw a long thin scar on his captor's neck, from a previous knife attack he surmised. He could smell booze, mixed with cigars on the Baron's breath. Tim shivered at the coldness in the man's eyes.

'I'll do my best to help her,' Tim affirmed, looking towards Raquel who smiled in return.

'You'd better! What do you need to do?' the Baron asked.

'I'll need to speak to Raquel and examine her. Does she speak Spanish?' Tim asked, more assertively as he moved from captive to clinician.

'No, but her sister Carolina does. Juan go and bring her,' the Baron instructed, in a tone that had to be obeyed.

Once Carolina arrived, Tim was allowed to sit down and speak to Raquel. She told him that she was eighteen years old and had been pregnant once before but that she had lost the baby after a long labour. Raquel was living in the city of Iquitos at the time. The baby was breech, coming feet first, and she was having a lot of difficulty so she was taken to the hospital but the baby became stuck. The doctors had to use forceps to pull the baby out but it was too late, the baby was dead. She was told that in future that if she wanted to have any more children then she would have an operation, a caesarean section.

'I'll have to examine you. Is there somewhere you can lie down?' Tim asked gently. He felt sorry for his young patient already; the Baron must have been twenty-five years older than the girl. Tim wondered why she had entered into such a relationship or if she had had any choice!

'There's a bed through there, use that,' the Baron interrupted curtly.

Tim examined his patient. He could feel his heart start to race as he contemplated finding the baby lying feet first again. To his horror, he realised the baby was lying across Raquel's abdomen and as she was due to give birth any day now there was no chance the baby would turn into the correct position. He examined her a second time just to be absolutely sure, but no, the baby was definitely a transverse lie.

Tim started to feel sick; she needed a surgical delivery. There was no way this mother would be able to deliver her baby on her own; if she was allowed to try, she and the child were very likely to die!

Tim stood up on shaky legs and returned to the main room of the lodge where he took a deep breath and stated, as emphatically, as he dare, 'Raquel will have to go to a hospital for surgery.'

'You mean Iquitos. No way. There's a warrant out for her arrest and mine. We aren't going anywhere near a hospital. Haven't you done this sort of operation before?' asked the Baron, impatiently.

'No, not on my own, but I have assisted the surgeon in a modern hospital.'

'You'd better come up with a solution gringo doctor,' the Baron said grabbing Tim round the neck. ''Cos if she dies, you die! Do you understand me? Take him away.'

Anxious and frightened at the predicament he was in Tim was man-handled back to his prison by Eduardo and another fighter.

'I hope you've the answer gringo doctor; don't forget, the Boss always keeps his word.'

Eduardo's parting comment had the desired affect and increased Tim's apprehension.

Rick was pacing about like a caged animal. Tim's cellmate was a weak looking man in his late forties, dark-haired, thinning on top, dressed in torn shorts and a sweat-stained, short-sleeved shirt. He had been roughed up a good deal by his kidnappers, as could be seen in his face: an obvious black eye and bruising to his jaw.

'Where have you been? Have you seen the Baron? Have you been to your patient yet?' Rick asked, anxiously. 'He's a lovely specimen of humanity isn't he?'

'Oh yes! He's such a great guy! I'm in a real fix. There's no way she's going to give birth to a live child. The baby is lying across the way instead of head down. She needs surgery to delivery the baby. How do I do that out here?' Tim replied, holding his head in his hands.

'Let's think it through. What would normally happen in the jungle? There must be some doctors around here, surely,' Rick asked, trying to help and calm his new friend.

'They've Ministry of Health midwives who visit some of the communities. If they think a mother has a very big baby or is likely to have a difficult birth she's advised to go to the hospital, but the nearest one is in the city of Iquitos. The village chief has some government money to pay for the riverboat trip, but often the woman won't go because she has other children that need to be looked after. To make matters worse, Raquel is wanted by the police so there's no way she's going near Iquitos,' Tim explained, despondently as he too paced around their prison.

'I thought there was a regional town near here. Isn't there a clinic there? Surely the doctor delivers babies?' Rick suggested, refusing to give up.

'Yeah, Intuto, but the doctor returned to Iquitos last month. I was kidnapped from a village near there,' Tim said, thoughtfully peering through the slats towards the Baron's lodge.

'Hey, wait a minute you could be right!' Tim continued. 'The clinic there has a small operating room. It looked so basic, I'd hardly call it an operating theatre but it is better than the floor of a lodge here; there should be some anaesthetics too. Please God let there be all the equipment I need. Rick this just might work, this has to work or I'm dead. I've never seen such an evil man as the Baron,' Tim exclaimed, with the excitement of a man who had just had his execution postponed to allow another hearing at the Appeal Court.

'Has a young doctor like you carried out this sort of operation before?' Rick said incredulously. 'Back in the States, our doctors are in their early thirties before they're let loose on patients.'

'I know, but it's a different system in the UK; our doctors graduate in their mid-twenties. I've assisted at a few such operations. But I've no choice, I have to attempt to operate, it's the only hope for Raquel, her baby and of course me. It is literally do or die!'

For the next few hours Tim and Rick were left undisturbed in their prison cell. Tim discovered that Rick had been working about ninety miles away, or so he thought, surveying an area of the jungle north west of the Rio Nanay. He explained that the government in Lima had recognised that their country had considerable oil and mineral reserves; opening up these deposits would add to the wealth of the nation. His expertise was welcomed by the Peruvians as he had travelled all over the world, assessing potential oil and gas fields for future exploration.

Rick told Tim that this area was very rich in oil but

unlike the usual places he had surveyed: deserts in Africa, Arctic and Antarctic ice caps this was a beautiful jungle region. His fear was that unless tight controls were kept on the oil companies, the Amazon jungle was in grave danger of being destroyed. The ancient way of life of the Amazonian people would vanish and there would be an ecological disaster that would have far reaching effects on the rest of the world. He believed that the government would start off with good intentions of protecting the rainforest and all its inhabitants but in reality, because the area is so remote, the work would be inadequately policed. Corrupt officials and 'get rich quick' companies would ruthlessly exploit the indigenous population.

'Have you considered why there are so many young girls around the cantina at the back of the compound?' Rick asked his young companion.

'I had noticed there seemed to be a lot considering how isolated this place is,' Tim replied, as he tried to work out what Rick was getting at.

'I'll bet these girls have been trafficked from another area of Peru, to keep the men folk happy after work. Look how young they are!' Rick offered, pointing to a group of girls walking back to the saloon.

'You're kidding. Right?'

'No, I've come across it before. The Peruvian police last year carried out a raid in the south of the country; a gold mine in the foothills of the Andes that was controlled by organised criminals. They did an early morning swoop and found forty girls between the ages of twelve and sixteen living in the most horrible conditions. The girls had been kidnapped from the slums in Arequipa and Puna region, thrown into the back of lorries and then driven for days over mountain passes to the gold mine. Once there, they were forced into prostitution by the gang leaders. The story was in one of the national papers; many of the girls were reunited with their parents but the police chief admitted they were just scraping the surface of the problem.'

'That's disgusting. They're just children!' Tim exclaimed, in disbelief.

'Sadly it goes on all over the world. In countries such as Cambodia or Vietnam for example, sometimes the parents are so poor the families become prey to organised criminals. The mother will borrow money to buy food to feed her children and when she can't repay, the criminals come and take her daughter to be used and abused in the sex industry,' Rick continued in a matter of fact tone.

'I've heard a bit about sex tourism in these Far Eastern countries,' Tim acknowledged.

'It's not just girls that are exploited you know. I have an African friend, Joseph, a human rights lawyer; he has told me of some other terrible things happening in his country. He investigated a diamond mine in the east of Africa, there he found boys of ten or eleven years who worked sixteen hours a day down in the mines; their small frames made them ideal for extracting the precious stones in narrow shafts. Frequently there would be a collapse and boys would be killed. Joseph discovered that many of these boys had been street boys who were kidnapped and trafficked from the cities to the mine; they had no hope of escape. My friend tried to bring a case against the company but when he returned with law enforcement officers all the boys had gone and no one on the site would testify against the owners; there was such a culture of fear and intimidation among the adult workforce.'

'Why is it always the children?' Tim asked, shaking his head. 'You've seen a lot as you've travelled the world. What else have you found out about this trafficking? I thought it was about drugs and arms, not human beings.'

'Some quite awful things really. My legal friend, Joseph, has lots of evidence. For example, he received information about children forced to work at a gold mine in a neighbouring state. He entered the gold mine area on several occasions, disguised as a truck driver, delivering supplies; he told me how shocked he was by what he saw. These were older boys who were thin and ill from lack of food; many were poisoned by the mercury used to extract the gold. Joseph learned that when they were too ill to work, they were just discarded into the jungle to fend for themselves. Again the lawyer tried to bring a case against the company but he found it impossible to persuade the local police to act. One night on his way back to his hotel he was set upon by three men who beat him up really badly; they told him to get back home before something worse happened to him and his family. He has put pressure on his government to do something about the exploitation of children in his country for many years now. Sadly, he said that it was an uphill struggle against the criminal gangs who have infiltrated everywhere in Africa, as well as many other countries of the world. These gangs have realised that using slaves means bigger profits.'

'That's terrible! I had no idea it was such a widespread problem,' Tim replied incredulously.

'As long as the poor are uneducated and unaware of their rights they'll always be vulnerable to traffickers. I bet you didn't know that human trafficking is the fastest growing international crime and of course the majority of victims are women and girls. The worst bit is that the girls in places like Cambodia are bought and sold by men from the United States and Europe,' Rick explained, determined to further his young friend's education.

'Please stop! It's disgusting,' Tim requested, holding his head in his hands again.

'Yip! Yet people try to tell me there's a God! How can a loving God allow such awful things to happen to innocent kids?' Rick asked.

'It's not God's fault,' Tim answered, softly. 'It's evil men. God intended humanity to live good lives, but we screwed up a long time ago!'

Rick continued to wander round the room, wringing his hands, his thoughts returning to his own predicament.

'What about us? This lot are going to kill me and probably you when they've finished using you; the US government won't pay for me. What about my wife, my girls? I won't see them again,' Rick mumbled, as he collapsed onto the only chair in the hut, in tears. Tim went over to comfort his new friend.

'Don't give up Rick. If we're going to survive we have to be strong. Have you eaten anything today?' Tim asked.

'How can I eat this rubbish? There are insects in the food and the bread is mouldy; it's disgusting!'

'We'll just have to break off the blue bits. If you don't eat, we've no chance of escaping,' Tim said, as he put his arm around the older man.

'Do they know you are a geologist?' Tim asked, changing the subject slightly.

'No, I don't think so. Just that I'm an American,' Rick replied in a faltering voice. 'A Yank, who is valuable to them.'

'Good, we might be able to buy some time. Maybe they could do with some expert help with the mining; that would get you out of here and give you a better chance to escape,' Tim suggested.

'Good thinking, Doc,' Rick replied, a bit more confidently. 'But you couldn't use an ex-army medic could you, when you go to Intuto to deliver the baby?'

'I could do with any help I can get! What did you do in the army?' Tim asked, as he began to formulate a plan.

'I was in the army reserves during the first Gulf war. I played the trumpet in the battalion band so my specialty, as most bandsmen, was evacuation of casualties from the frontline back to the field hospital. I used to know how to put up an intravenous drip, splint fractured limbs, airway protection and all that sort of stuff. I joined the reserves while I was at university for a bit of variety but I guess I never thought I would be called up. I saw some pretty nasty stuff, but that was a long time ago now.'

'It'll come back to you; I need all the help I can get,' Tim replied. 'And that's what I need to convince the Baron!'

Tim had just finished speaking when they heard footsteps coming towards the hut. The door was quickly opened and there stood Eduardo, Tim's kidnapper.

'Hi gringo Doc, the Boss wants you to take a look at his lady. She's in some sort of pain,' Eduardo reported. 'Come! Now!'

As they walked across to the Baron's lodge, Tim asked Eduardo where all the medical equipment had gone as he needed it now. Eduardo barked off an order to one of the sentries who disappeared off. Tim was anxious to look through his textbooks for some reassurance about the technical side of a caesarean section; after all he had only ever assisted, which was quite different from being the surgeon. How he wished he had paid more attention!

Raquel was lying on her back on the bed, feeling faint and writhing in pain. Tim immediately rolled her on to her side to take the weight of the baby off her large abdominal blood vessel; this simple act of correct positioning allowed more blood to return to her heart and brain and improve her blood pressure. The young woman felt better very quickly, which reassured her that Tim knew what he was doing.

Tim sat with his patient for half an hour; Eduardo had returned with Tim's rucksack so he was able to listen to the baby's heart rate with his stethoscope and check Raquel's blood pressure. All was normal, so far so good. Tim rechecked the baby's position just to confirm his original findings; the foetus was definitely lying across the mother's womb. Raquel's contractions were quite erratic and not fully established; some twenty minutes, others twenty-five with only slight discomfort for her, but Tim knew this would change very quickly, especially as this was her second pregnancy. He smiled at the frightened woman and then tried to reassure her, through her sister's translation, that he would do all he could to deliver a healthy baby. The young doctor knew that baby was completely innocent, regardless of the wicked activities of the father, and that he was going to use all his medical skills to save mother and babe.

As Tim sat waiting for the next contraction, the Baron rushed through.

'What's happening gringo Doc?' he asked, as gruffly as ever.

'The labour has started, but as I tried to tell you earlier, there's a problem. The baby is lying across Raquel's tummy and not head down the way it should be. She'll not be able to deliver the baby without an operation,' Tim said with the authority of someone who knew what he was talking about. He knew he couldn't allow any doubt to show, if he was going to save this mother and child.

'Can't you turn the child around?' the Baron asked, with a hint of concern in his voice, which surprised Tim.

'Can we speak about this next door? Raquel needs to rest,' Tim said as he rose from the bedside.

The Baron turned and walked to the other room; Tim followed.

'What are you going to do then?' the older man demanded to know, glaring at the doctor.

Tim could actually see the concern in this hard man's face. Perhaps he really was capable of love; maybe he did love this young woman and the baby she was carrying. The doctor explained to his captor that the only way the mother and baby could be saved was by opening up her abdomen, a caesarean section, and removing the baby from the womb and it couldn't be done here; it would have to be carried out in a hospital. The Baron just laughed, the nearest hospital was an hour away by plane and he didn't have an aircraft he told Tim.

'What about Intuto? There's a clinic there and there's a small basic operating room. There should be medicines in the pharmacy too. It's Raquel's and the baby's best chance!' Tim suggested to the Baron, almost pleading with him.

'There's an army patrol group there, remember the boat that attacked my guys the other night. It's too risky!' the Baron retorted, without hesitation.

'How far is it? No more than an hour by fast boat? Perhaps you need to create a diversion that'll take the patrol boats south towards Berlin. Then we could sneak into Intuto while the army boys are downstream,' Tim suggested, hardly believing his own words, advising a crook like the Baron.

'You really want to help Raquel, don't you gringo Doc?' the Baron declared, rather surprised. 'And you think fast; I like that in a man. You should come and work for me, I'll make you rich!' he continued, with a wry smile on his face.

'You might be in trouble with the law, but Raquel and your baby deserve a chance,' Tim replied righteously.

'I like your plan. We'll leave in half an hour. Get Raquel and Carolina ready to travel. Roberto here will watch over you. Just remember, if you try anything, we will kill you!'

'I need a nurse to help during the operation. Do you have anyone who is trained here?' Tim asked, hoping desperately for a negative answer.

'Eduardo, do you know of any one?' the Baron asked his second in command.

'No.' replied Eduardo, shaking his head.

'I was talking to Rick, the American. He was a medic in the army; he would know what to do. I can't do the operation myself,' Tim declared adamantly.

'You'll have to manage somehow! Use Carolina,' the Baron suggested, becoming impatient.

'She'll have to take care of the baby. Would you be able to hold retractors then?' Tim asked in all seriousness.

'No! Take the American! Eduardo get him and be sure and tell him what happens if he tries anything,' the Baron conceded.

Chapter 12

Fateful Incision

By early evening Tim, Rick and his patient were in the clinic at Intuto. The gang had executed the cunning plan. One fast boat full of fighters left the camp, about half an hour before the main party of three boats. This advance party was the decoy; its job was to head downstream as far as the village of Berlin, shoot the place up a bit and to set fire to a couple of huts. The bandits hoped that radio contact would be made and patrol boats despatched from Intuto to Berlin. They were not disappointed.

Once they were in the fast boat, Tim and Rick were blindfolded; Raquel and Carolina travelled in another boat. The journey was much quicker with a strong river current and no interceptions from the military. The little flotilla arrived just to the north of Intuto within the hour, just as darkness fell. Lights were switched off and engines silenced while the party waited for the patrol boats to take the bait. The two captives, blindfolds now removed, watched anxiously with the others. If spotted by the army it would have meant another wild chase which would have put them both, and of course the mother to be, at risk.

They didn't have to wait long, much to Tim's relief;

he was growing increasingly concerned for his patient. First one and then another army craft sped off down river and from the silhouettes each packed with soldiers. Tim groaned as he realised that young men would probably die that night, all because of the Baron's greed and criminality.

The boats proceeded to the jetty at Intuto. The group disembarked like a normal visiting party looking for a bed for the night; the fighters with weapons concealed, strolled up the jetty to the town. Raquel, helped by Carolina and Tim, was buckling with pain as she struggled up the slope to the main square; her contractions were intensifying and coming about every five minutes. The Baron and three other of his men walked ahead, behind came Rick carrying Tim's rucksack with Eduardo at his shoulder. The group turned off the main street towards the clinic. Suddenly the town was plunged into darkness as the street lights failed. Tim wondered if the town's generator had run out of diesel, or if one of the Baron's men had temporarily disabled it.

Eduardo and his men made short work of the security at the clinic. Once inside, the building was secured with armed sentries in position. Unexpectedly in one of the back rooms, Federico was writing a report. He was man-handled through to the clinic room where Tim and Rick were searching for equipment.

'Don't hurt him!' Tim yelled at the terrorist. 'He'll be able to help us; he'll know where everything is.'

The fighter looked at the Baron for confirmation and released his grip on the terrified young man.

'What's your name?' asked Tim trying to make out he had never met the nurse before. If the Baron had realised that Tim knew of the nurse he would quickly see that there was no need to bring Rick.

'Federico, I'm the nurse here,' the young man said, catching on to the situation very quickly, much to Tim's relief.

'You must be the one who was up river, doing vaccinations, when I was here last week. I'm Dr Tim. We've a pregnant girl here who needs emergency surgery if we are to save her baby. Have you helped with this before? Do you have anaesthetic drugs so we can put her to sleep?'

'Yes, I've helped before, but not usually at the point of a gun,' the nurse replied, looking anxiously at Eduardo's machine gun.

'You can see that we have no choice in the matter, but there can be no guns in the operating room,' Tim said, turning to the Baron for approval.

'Get on with it; Raquel is in a lot of pain now. Remember if you try anything or this baby dies, Eduardo knows what to do!' the Baron declared, with a look that told Tim he meant every word he said.

Federico staying late that night was a God-send Tim decided. The nurse knew where everything was: the anaesthetic drugs and equipment, surgical drapes, the resuscitation tubes and blankets for the newborn; he even sent Eduardo to the emergency generator. Everything was worn but adequate under the circumstances.

Tim reassessed his patient; she was almost exhausted, her contractions were very strong and painful now. To make matters worse, as Tim listened to the baby's heart rate he found it was slowing right down following each contraction; this was a sign that the baby was stressed and needed to be delivered urgently. The medic knew he had to act fast to save this foetus. Federico and Rick prepared Raquel on the operating table. Rick was able to put up the intravenous drip at first attempt much to his delight.

Fortunately Federico had assisted the other jungle doctors during surgery and so had experience of using the anaesthetics. Once Tim had put Raquel to sleep, Federico would keep her unconscious throughout the procedure.

As Tim and Rick hurriedly scrubbed their hands, each thought of the enormous task that lay in front of them. The young surgeon knew he was not only fighting for the life of mother and child but also his own life and probably Rick and Federico's too. He knew that the Baron was like all psychopaths: ruthless, cold and brutal. If the baby died there might be no end to the retribution that would follow.

Raquel lay quietly on the operating table anaesthetised now, free of pain. Once the abdomen was cleaned and the drapes were in place Tim picked up the scalpel to make the incision. He had been rehearsing the operation as they had travelled down in the fast boat; surprisingly he had found the blindfold helpful as he was able to concentrate and take his mind through the entire procedure not once, but three times. He carefully made his skin incision along her midline taking care to miss her navel; one third above her tummy button two thirds below, the best type of incision in an emergency like this and with his level of experience. Raquel didn't flinch, her sleep was deep enough.

Tim could see the pregnant womb bulging like an over-inflated football beneath the skin wound. With Rick's help he widened the wound and packed gauze around the uterus so that none of the birth fluid would leak into Raquel's abdominal cavity. This done he checked that Carolina was ready with towels to receive the baby then he made the incision into the thick muscle of the womb. He knew he had to be quick; he slipped his fingers into the uterus to protect the baby from his knife, and then with the calmness of a seasoned surgeon he extended the incision to reveal the legs of the infant. Even the sharp intake of breath, followed by the large thud when Carolina fell to the ground with shock, failed to distract the surgeon; he knew this baby's life depended on his swift action. Federico dashed to Carolina's aid and laid her out, flat on the floor.

Tim's hand was now inside the womb locating the feet before gently delivering the foetus. A very blue, wrinkly baby was now swinging from his hand; the quick traditional slap on the buttocks from his other hand had the desired effect. The baby let out a cry and took its first breath, much to everyone's huge relief. Tim clamped and cut the cord before passing the little boy to Rick who had now taken over Carolina's duty.

Tim now turned his attention to Raquel.

'Have you given her the injection to contract her uterus, Federico?' he asked assertively.

'Yes, I gave it as soon as baby was born,' the jungle nurse said with a confident smile.

'Great! Now for the after birth,' Tim muttered as he searched round the uterus for the placenta. 'Are the mother's blood pressure and heart rate OK?' Tim asked his nurse.

'She's fine,' Federico replied, 'pulse and blood pressure are good.'

After a further thirty minutes, Tim put in the final stitch to his patient's abdominal wound. Carolina, who had made a full recovery from her faint, was holding a very pink infant, wrapped in a blanket. She brought the baby over to Tim.

'You did a terrific job. You should take the baby to the Baron,' she suggested, as she handed the infant over to the surgeon.

Tim ripped off his surgical gloves and reached for the child.

'Thank you God! He's just beautiful. Thank you Lord for making everything work out just fine. Let's take you to see your father,' he said to the babe, as he walked out of the worst operating room he had ever worked in.

The Baron rushed over towards the doctor to take hold of his little one. Tim saw a glimpse of anxiety on the bandit's face.

'Is it a boy?' the Baron asked, with a definite nervousness in his voice that Tim could hardly believe.

Tim nodded.

'It's a boy! A boy! My first son, my first child. Eduardo, look at my boy!' the Baron said as he walked over to his friend showing off his precious son.

'Raquel is still asleep but should be awake in about twenty minutes,' Tim told the gangster.

'When will she be ready to travel? We need to get out of here before the patrol boats return,' Eduardo reminded Tim, while the Baron cooed over his child.

'She needs to rest and feed the baby. It would be best to wait until morning,' Tim advised.

'No! No chance we must be out of here within the hour,' the Baron dictated, returning to his hard man mentality.

'But! Raquel will not be fit by then,' Tim cautioned hoping to give the young woman the best chance he could.

'Then you and the American will carry her. Eduardo, see to it! Dispose of that nurse; we don't want anyone to know we were here,' the Baron instructed, with his usual ruthlessness.

Tim shuddered at what he had just heard. This man was an animal; Federico's life didn't matter to him it was just another commodity, just like the young girls in the cantina, something to be bought and sold, used and abused.

'I'll need Federico to help me with Raquel's wound dressing. He has the skills I don't have. We should take him with us; at least until the girl's wound is healed,' Tim requested, hoping to buy time for the nurse.

'Sure, we can keep him a few more days. Come to think of it a nurse could be quite useful at the camp,' the Baron conceded, much to Tim's surprise.

It was four in the morning when the flotilla left the jetty at Intuto. The captives were blindfolded again, despite Tim's protestations. They were in the lead boat with Eduardo, a young Columbian at the helm and one other gunman with a submachine gun at the rear. The women and baby were in the middle boat with the Baron. The third fast boat was at the back of the convoy with six heavily armed fighters. Fortunately there was no sign of the patrol boats; Tim could only conclude that the decoy attack had worked, but the potential loss of lives made him shudder once more. On the journey back, Tim tried to work out when they turned from the Rio Tigre and how many tributaries they followed but it was impossible in the darkness.

His thoughts turned to what was going to happen to him now the baby had been safely brought into the world. What was going to happen to Rick and Federico? The Baron was an evil, violent man. How could anyone be caressing his newborn son, promising him the very best in life and then without even taking breath, command that another's life should be taken and for no other reason than he was in the wrong place at the wrong time?

Then, without any warning, the first boat leapt in the air and threw its occupants into the river. Tim ripped off his blindfold as he floundered in the water. He could hear the shouts of the others splashing around trying to make it to the shore. The Baron's crew realised what had happened and came over to the stricken vessel. The helmsman put on the search light only to be roared at by the Baron to put it out in case of patrols, but they managed to pick up one survivor. In the brief moment of light, Tim spotted Federico panicking and floundering only a couple of metres from him. Tim struck out to reach the nurse, grabbed him from behind and kicked for the shore. The current was taking them downstream but with each kick Tim drew closer to the riverbank. Finally he managed to grab a low branch and haul himself and Federico onto the bank. Federico was coughing and spluttering, but glad to be alive.

The pair quickly realised this was an opportunity not to be missed. As quietly as possible they moved away from the bank and hid under vegetation but they could still hear the shouts of the Baron.

'Find the American! He's worth a lot to us. Don't waste time on the other two. The current is so strong the camen will soon dispose of their bodies. What did you say? Eduardo is dead! Stupid fool he should have seen the log!' the Baron roared to his men.

'We can't see anyone Boss,' said one of the fighters, peering into the darkness.

'Here! Help me! I'm here!' Rick shouted as he clung to the far side of the upturned boat. He was a poor swimmer and he knew to try to swim to the bank would mean certain death. The gang quickly moved in with their boat and grabbed Rick. He was safe, at least for now.

'Good! Now we must go; the mosquitoes are eating me alive. At first light we'll send some men back to look for the other two, just in case they made it to the bank. Not much chance the gringo doctor will survive the jungle anyway, but if he does, he knows too much. Let's go!' the Baron barked, more forcefully than ever.

Chapter 13

Aiming High

The alarm clock brought Katie back from the plantation in Alabama where the slaves were picking cotton. The young journalist sat bolt upright in bed, rubbing her eyes and wondering how she had managed to dream about slaves. Then she remembered her late night internet search. Surely slaves don't still exist? she questioned.

Katie bounded out of bed, she had slept in! She desperately needed to impress her editor today and being late would not be a good start. What would Sandra make of Laura's story? Katie wondered as she wolfed down her muesli. Maybe she wouldn't want to publish it without real names and addresses; perhaps the editor wouldn't want to risk *The Herald*'s reputation with such a story, Katie doubted.

When Katie parked her car outside the office she realised she couldn't remember the journey she had just made; she desperately hoped she hadn't missed any speed cameras! She had been so busy going over in her mind again and again what she was going to say at the meeting with her editor. She didn't want to muck up and risk letting Laura and her mother down. Suddenly, Katie knew that this assignment really mattered to her!

Sandra was tied up with one thing after another so it was over an hour before Katie could meet with her; a nerve wracking time for the student who spent the time checking her notes and looking over all she had learnt the night before from her research.

'So you've an interesting piece you want to discuss. Have you written it up yet?' the editor asked briskly.

'No I haven't because I have some queries about the subject matter,' Katie replied, somewhat nervously.

'Fire away. You have ten minutes until I have to meet with the subeditors,' Sandra instructed.

Katie explained as concisely as she could the encounter with Laura and her mother; Sandra didn't interrupt once. The older woman played thoughtfully with her pen, listening intently. Once Katie was finished Sandra turned and looked out of the window in contemplation. Katie's heart pounded in her chest in anticipation. Had she been clear enough? Had she gone on too long? Had she let Laura down? All these doubts filled her mind in an instant.

'I can understand the anonymity, as it's such a harrowing story, and it could be a problem for us. But this story deeply troubles me; I heard of a similar case last year in Liverpool, but the prosecution was dropped by the courts through lack of witnesses. It had all the same features as the account you've just given,' Sandra commented, obviously moved by all she had just heard.

'Last night I spent hours on the internet and found a newspaper article of a court case in Newcastle; it was dropped, too, through lack of evidence,' Katie replied.

'Right, I have to go. Katie we are definitely going to do something with this but I don't think it'll be in this daily; this is more of a feature. Go and write it as a feature article for say, a Sunday magazine. Take your time, do some more research. This is Wednesday, too late for this Sunday's papers anyway. We'll aim for a week Sunday. Have the piece ready by Friday afternoon; I'll give you an hour then, three until four,' Sandra said as she took a pen and cleared the session in her dairy. 'This is good stuff! Well done, see you Friday.'

Sandra dashed through the doorway heading for the newsroom and her awaiting subeditors. Katie didn't get a chance to say that this was her last week at *The Herald*. By Friday evening Katie would have finished her placement, but she was so stunned by Sandra's positive response that holidays were the last thing on her mind. Meeting up with her parents in London the next week was now 'on hold', this assignment was far too important!

Returning to her desk, Katie sat for a while and thought over everything Sandra had said. Did she really say a Sunday paper magazine? How would she manage to get an article published in something so high profile? If so it would have to be Sandra's name at the bottom otherwise there would be no hope of publication. Who has ever heard of Katie Baxter, Investigative Journalist? Sounds good she thought, chuckling to herself. Oh how she wished she could phone Tim and tell him what was going on. Katie and Tim were very close and always had been since their ordeal in the Amazon. Katie would frequently confide in her big brother or ask his advice. She missed him, after all it was unusual for her not to be able to contact him but she knew he was 'healing the sick' deep in the jungle. Her thoughts were interrupted by John.

'Why are you looking so pleased with yourself? Count-ing down the days until you leave and start your holidays, you lucky girl?' John asked in his usual teasing way 'I've another six weeks of this grind until my vacation with my beloved in sunny Wales.'

Over the last three weeks Katie had come to like John. He was all talk and totally devoted to his girl, a young constable in the Met in London. John adored her and couldn't wait to meet up with her whenever her off duty allowed.

'Oh by the way, how did your mystery encounter go yesterday? Closing the "Ladies" in the High Street then are they?' John enquired.

'It was an interesting meeting with a mother and teenage daughter. I'm just about to write a piece for Sandra,' Katie said, trying not to give too much away.

'Is this an assessment before you leave?' John asked, wondering why Sandra had asked for a piece from the student.

Katie's heart skipped a beat. Surely, Sandra meant what she said about publishing the piece; it wasn't just an exercise?

'Possibly. I suppose I'd better get on with it then,' Katie said, trying to shake off John so she could get started.

The young student spent the next two days writing and rewriting her article until she was happy with it. She counted five drafts before she was satisfied it was as good as she could make it. Her evenings were spent researching trafficking and modern-day slavery. Reputable websites such as the United Nations and others gave Katie a frightening insight into the world of the enslaved in the twenty-first century. Estimates of twenty-seven million slaves worldwide, the majority women and children; how can this be? she wondered.

The trainee couldn't understand how, in a modern world

with organisations such as the United Nations, which was established to ensure human rights for all of the world's citizens, that these inhumanities still went on. Worse still she discovered that over a million children were believed to be trafficked for the sex trade and of course she had heard first-hand evidence of this happening on her doorstep.

Katie discovered that one of the world news organisations had done an enormous amount of research on this global problem. She learnt that the driving force behind enslavement and trafficking was the criminal underworld. Up until recently most international criminal gangs were involved in drug trafficking and gun running but now they had turned to slavery as the financial rewards were much greater. Globally it was thought trafficking of people was worth thirty-two billion dollars. Katie couldn't even imagine how huge that was. The other big factor was that law enforcement in the area of trafficking was weak; criminals were not adequately pursued and sentences were inadequate. The trainee reporter couldn't believe it when she read that someone convicted of trafficking cocaine would be imprisoned for longer than someone found guilty of trafficking young girls into prostitution.

At times Katie found things she uncovered really harrowing but she was also encouraged by the stories she read of survivors and how with the help of specific charities they were rebuilding their lives. She came across websites set up by young people in Asia, America and the UK; each group filled with determination to stamp out the degrading practice of enslavement and helping to restore the victims to a normal life. Katie became even more determined to join the fight.

Friday lunchtime Katie received an email from Sandra asking to see the draft article before their meeting. Fortunately Katie was well organised so she fired off the document by return. All she had to do now was try and eat some lunch and hope that she had put the story across well enough.

To Katie's surprise Sandra was free, as promised, at three o'clock on the dot.

'Katie, I've given a great deal of thought to this and reading your feature has just reinforced my decision. I phoned my old boss at the *Sunday Tribune*, Graham Anderson, and told him about your interview with Laura and her mother. He's interested! Your draft was first class, by the way, but will require a few tweaks here and there,' Sandra explained.

'Wow! The *Sunday Tribune*! Are you sure they'll run with it?' Katie asked in utter disbelief.

'No I'm not. But Graham's a decent guy. I've taken the liberty of sending off the draft to him so he has the facts. His usual style would be to respond before the end of the day,' Sandra said, encouragingly.

'Are you remembering that my attachment finishes this afternoon, Sandra?' Katie asked, not sure what to expect from her boss.

'Already! Your four weeks finished already? Mmm! That's a bit of a problem. You should really be employed here at *The Herald* and be available next week, ready for any developments, after we run this story. Here we go, Graham's sent an email, he must be trying to finish early today. Let's have a look,' Sandra said, as she opened up the email on her laptop.

Katie's stomach was in knots! Her hands were sweaty, her heart racing and her fingers trembling. What if this man, Graham, did publish my feature? How brilliant that would be to have Laura's story out there for all to read. Please God let him say yes!

'Hey! Hey! He loves it! He wants to run it next weekend as he has another similar article going out; this one is on trafficking of young women from Eastern Europe into the brothels of Paris, London, Rome and other European cities,' Sandra relayed excitedly to her young colleague.

'That's so exciting!' Katie said, allowing herself to relax just a little.

'He would like some photographs. That could be a problem. Do you have any ideas about pictures, Katie? Oh! And we definitely need you here for the next two weeks. Can you do it? I'll clear it with HR,' Sandra asked, expecting Katie to agree under the circumstances.

'I was going up to London to see my parents; they are home on leave from Mumbai. They'll definitely understand. My mother is an investigative journalist and her special interest is cases involving the abuse of the rights of young women and girls,' Katie explained. 'In India, she is never short of stories.'

'So that's where the passion comes from. I picked it up in your article, that's what makes it so good; this story has had a huge effect on you I think,' Sandra commented.

'I just don't think what happened to Laura was fair: the grooming, then the violations, the cruelty and the failure of the authorities to act. The thought that there are other young people, boys as well as girls, out there being exploited for money just appals me. We have to warn parents and young people that there are horrible predators out there,' Katie replied, getting worked up.

'You'll make a good journalist, Katie. I've watched

you over the last few weeks, you work hard and anything mediocre is not acceptable to you. You remind me of myself when I was young, desperate to change the world for the better. The trouble is once you get up the ladder into management, with owners of the newspaper breathing down your neck, it's all about selling papers, so you have to give the readers what they want to read. If we get a juicy story about a 'celeb' we run with it or if a politician makes a fool of himself we print it! But this grooming story has to be told; pieces like this remind me why I chose a career in journalism,' Sandra said, thoughtfully.

'Thank you, I always try to do my best.'

'I'll put some corrections and suggestions on your first draft. You sort them out and email them to me over the weekend. What about pictures?' Sandra asked, suddenly remembering.

'What about a shot of the cathedral café where we held the interview?' Katie suggested.

'I don't think it would paint a sinister enough picture. It might do as one, among others,' Sandra mused.

'What if we set up a photo of a girl, around Laura's age, sitting at a table looking out of a window? It would have to be a back view though,' Katie suggested trying to get into the mood of the article.

'Now we're getting somewhere. If it was a black and white shot with a city skyline glimpsed through the window that could work. I'll phone Bob, he's the photographer for the job and he'll have just the right girl for the picture. I'll let him know the story,' Sandra said assertively, as she reached out for the phone.

'I'll see you first thing Monday morning. I'll send you the corrected draft before the end of the day; hopefully I'll manage to do a bit of work on it this evening. The deadline for the *Tribune* is noon on Wednesday, so we've a bit of time yet. By the way, this feature will have your name on the bottom! Have a good weekend.

'Hi Bob...' Sandra said, as she swivelled round in her chair indicating to Katie it was time to go home.

Chapter 14

More Hostility

The roar of the remaining two fast boats faded into the distance as the Baron and his fighters made their way back to the camp. The two young men lay in the undergrowth and tried to take in all that had just happened. They began to relax to the noise of the jungle: the insects, the croaking frogs, the distant barks; a welcome change from the persistent loud drone of the boat engines. After a few minutes they had recovered sufficiently to think about their next move.

'We have to get out of here!' Tim said. 'They're coming back at first light to look for us. They realise that I know too much about what's going on. Have you any idea where we are, Federico?'

'No. I have only been in Intuto for the past month. I haven't been northeast of the town before. Previously I worked in Libertad on the Nanay River; I was there for two years working with the local clinic doctor,' Federico answered, feeling safe enough to sit up and peer across the river, which glinted in the few shafts of moonlight that had squeezed through the cloud cover.

'That's why you were so good in the operating room last

night. I couldn't have done it without you, amigo,' Tim declared. 'We need to get out of here but it would be best if we wait until the moon is clear of the clouds so we can see a bit better. I'd hate to stand on a snake! Any suggestions which way we should go?'

'We must get away from the bank and go inland because the Baron's men are going to go up and down the river looking for any sign of us. I think they'll kill us on sight,' Federico cautioned. 'I know it makes sense to follow the river back downstream but that would be suicidal in my opinion. We have to take our chance in the jungle, for now at any rate. Dawn can't be that far off, maybe an hour, maybe less.'

'Yes, you're right. We'll head into the forest, at least until sunrise, and then find somewhere to hide and rest up. But I agree, to get back to Intuto we'll need to return to the river, unless we find a community with a canoe who know the way to the town,' Tim replied. He stood up and ran his hands over his limbs to dislodge the insects that had attached themselves to his skin. 'These leeches are driving me mad!' he moaned.

'But we won't be safe in Intuto. The Baron's men come in regularly for supplies. I recognised Eduardo last night as soon as I saw him; he collected some malaria tablets from the pharmacy the first week I was in town. You don't forget a man like that, such menacing body language. Do you think they bothered to take his corpse back to the camp for a proper burial?' Federico queried.

'I can't imagine they did. I've never come across such a hard man as the Baron. The day I arrived Miguel pointed out the strangers in the town; they just looked suspicious. Miguel was right to be wary of them,' Tim remarked.

'But if we get back to Intuto we can go to the army and tell them what's going on. Hopefully they'll believe us and mount a mission to rescue Rick. Not that I could lead them back there; surely they must have access to a spotter plane for work like that,' Tim continued.

'I don't think so, I haven't seen any planes up this way,' the nurse said.

'Of course it's not just Rick, there are girls and workers held captive in the camp; we must do something for them.'

'Why are there children in the camp?' Federico asked.

'They are forced to work in the mine or the cantina. Rick told me that the boys are treated abysmally: half starved, beaten if they don't work hard enough and shot if they try to escape. I've seen some very young girls round the saloon; I shudder to think what life is like for them,' Tim replied, as he leant against a branch waiting for the cloud to clear completely.

Ten minutes later and the two young men began to fight their way through the thick undergrowth. It was hard going until they stumbled upon a hunter's trail. By then dawn had arrived, the sun's rays filtered through the high canopy producing a marvellous scene around them. Tim could hear the chatter of the monkeys high in the trees as they fled from the intruders who had invaded their idyllic world; he wondered if they were tamarins but they were too far in front to get a proper look at them. The path was marshy and slippery in places and at times, it was hard to keep upright.

As the morning drew on, the sun's rays grew stronger and the temperature rose, Tim and Federico began to tire. They urgently needed to find water and some food. Federico was the first to spot some fruit but it wasn't any that Tim recognised. The pair tucked into their prize, the sugary content gave them much needed energy. Fortified they took to the track once more pushing on as fast and as quietly as they could.

Federico, who led the way, was more confident now with the improved light and a path to follow, but suddenly he stopped and listened.

'Listen! Do you hear that? Sounds like animals screeching, behind us to the left!' he asked, anxiously.

'Yeah! There it is again. There not reacting to us, maybe there's a big cat! The Baron's men can't be back here already, could they?' Tim queried, as he crouched down.

'Maybe it's a hunting party. I've heard that the Mica people live in this area. I've never met them as they've refused any help from the government. I've heard they have very powerful medicine men who dictate to the tribe,' Federico explained. 'Last year the Intuto doctor was instructed by the Ministry of Health in Iquitos to make contact with the tribe. He and his nurse were treated very badly by the Mica, they were held against their will for three days. Fortunately the doctor had spoken to the army captain about his concerns before he left, so when they didn't return a heavily armed patrol rescued them. No shots were fired but people say it was this incident that made the doctor decide to leave Intuto and return to civilisation.'

'I guess they must have really spooked the medic. What about the nurse? Did he leave for the same reason?' Tim asked, feeling even more uneasy.

'Yes'.

'If it's them they won't be too keen to see a gringo either. Maybe we should keep going, that way,' Tim suggested, as he pointed away to the right.

The two men continued quickly along the path, which as luck would have it veered to the right anyway. They'd made good progress, so they thought, when the route funnelled up a slope through a channel of dense trees on either side. Tim was keenly aware of the silence that had fallen and that they were very vulnerable to both hunters and wild animals; there was nowhere to run except back down the path. The track curved to the left and just as they rounded the corner three Indians stood in their way with spears raised. The boys turned to retreat only to be met by another three natives, blocking the path. They were, indeed, trapped!

The hunters were wearing loincloths and headbands decked with highly coloured bird feathers; they were covered in facial paint and white stripes on their arms. Tim thought they looked fierce and very threatening. The two captives were signalled to fall into line and to follow the warriors. There was no choice.

As they drudged on in the heat, sweat streaming into his eyes, Tim wondered what was next. At least he was thankful it hadn't been the Baron's men who had found them because he knew that they would have died in a hail of bullets, but if the hunters were the Mica, maybe that wasn't too clever either! After a half hour's forced march the group came to a river. Three of the warriors dived into the water and then indicated to their prisoners to do the same. The river was shaded by the trees so the water was cool and refreshing. Tim and Federico were so ready for a drink. Tim looked up from the river but couldn't see the other three hunters and then he spotted them coming downstream in two dug-out canoes.

'At least we'll be able to rest for a bit. These guys know

how to march through the jungle!' Federico said, immersed up to his armpits in the refreshing cool waters.

'I'm not sure how much more I could have taken in this heat, especially on a near empty stomach,' Tim replied to his friend when he surfaced, sweeping his wet hair back from his face.

The hunters allowed Tim and Federico to drink their fill before directing them to the canoes. Federico had tried speaking to them in the Spanish and the local dialect but the hunters didn't seem to understand. This convinced Tim that they must be of the reclusive Mica tribe, although so far they had treated them well.

The canoes hugged the bank as they paddled through some of the most beautiful scenery on the planet, Tim thought. Seated cross-legged in the middle of the first boat, he watched as birds with beautiful, brightly coloured feathers flew gracefully in formation and the small marmosets played about in the trees close to the bank; he found himself beginning to relax just a little.

After half an hour they arrived at a village community on the banks of the river. They were hustled into the main hut, probably the chief's. A young man of about eighteen came over and spoke to them in pigeon Spanish. He said that the chief was away to another village but would be back at first light. The boy said that he knew that the gringo was from the gold mine and that the chief would not be happy about this. Once the youth finished speaking the hunters took Tim and Federico to a small hut which was obviously used as the village jail; it had thick wooden bars on the windows and the door was firmly locked behind them. There was nothing on the floor for them to sleep on but in the corner was some water and food.

'At least they feed condemned men here,' Tim said, trying to lighten the moment.

'Did you understand everything the hunter said?' Federico asked 'It's not looking good.'

'I agree. They know about the gold mine. But I'm not sure if they think we are part of the gang or if somehow they know we've escaped and that they're going to return us to the Baron!' Tim answered. 'Do you think we could break out from here?'

'Maybe, but I'm sure there's a guard or two outside,' Federico cautioned.

'Yeah, there're two alright. These guys would track us down before we got very far anyhow. I'm starved, let's have a look at this food first and then think things over. Looks like another comfortable night on the sprung mattress,' Tim said, sarcastically.

The two men sat down to eat the food of yuca and small bits of fish. It was remarkably tasty but Tim put that down to the fact that he hadn't eaten properly since the feast, at Nueva Casa. Once they had finished eating the two stretched out on the floor to ease their aching limbs.

'Is Tim a common name in your country?' Federico asked the young doctor.

'I suppose it is,' Tim agreed as he lay looking up at the thatched roof wondering if there were any bats up there.

'It's just I came across a gringo boy called Tim about ten years ago,' the Peruvian continued.

'Was he with his family on holiday?' Tim asked. 'Where did you meet him?'

'In Iquitos, he was with his young sister. I think she was called Kay or something like that,' the nurse replied, as he watched a line of ants march across a beam above his head.

'Katie, was it Katie?' Tim enquired, as he sat bolt upright with anticipation.

'Yes, that was it. Katie. The children were being chased by police,' Federico said, as he too sat up with excitement. 'The police thought they were street kids so as usual they had set the dogs on them. My friend Andres and I went to help them.'

'Federico! Of course. I knew there was something about you, but I couldn't put my finger on it. Are you Rico?' Tim said with total excitement.

'Yes, I'm Rico.'

'What happened to you? Why didn't you go back to Gilberto, the "soup man"? We thought you were dead. You saved our lives!' Tim questioned as he reached out and embraced the young man he had been trying to track down for years. Tim had given him up for dead.

'It's a long story but I guess we've plenty of time tonight,' Rico replied as he propped himself up against the wall of the hut.

The Peruvian continued, 'The night after you were rescued we went back to the bridge where the "soup man" came, but there were policemen everywhere so we had to turn back.'

'You did try to come back to Gilberto for food, I knew you would,' Tim interrupted excitedly. 'So what happened to you?'

'On our way back to the hideout, a police patrol car spotted us and chased after us, but we managed to give it the slip when we scooted down a man-hole to our den, in the sewer. The next day one of the younger boys was sick with fever. I knew he needed something to eat and I couldn't bear the thought of him dying so soon after

Andres, so I risked going to the market in Belen to steal some food for him,' Rico explained, head bowed wringing his hands.

In the gloom of the cell, Tim watched Rico change from confident adult to nervous street boy before his eyes. He knew that in his mind Rico could see his sick friend and hear the noise of the busy Belen market place. Tim reached across to steady his friend and encourage him to continue the story.

'I'd managed to grab some bread from a baker's stall but two security men saw me and chased me through the streets. I'm not clear what happened next but I think I ran down a street by the river and it was there that the men caught up with me. They must have beaten me so much that I passed into unconsciousness. I remember waking up watching two black vultures walking on the other side of the street. I could see them through my misty eyes and thought this must be the end, I'm going to die. Two men walked by, scaring the birds away as they passed. The men didn't even stop to look at me. They were followed by an old woman who shuffled past; she looked down, muttered something and she too walked by.

I lay there pleading with your God, Tim, to help me or let me die quickly. Do you remember we talked about your God when my friend Andres died in the sewer? You said that God loved people, even street boys, but I didn't believe you. If He did why would He leave us to be treated like rats: hated and abused by everyone?' Rico asked as he lifted his gaze towards Tim, but before the doctor could answer to defend his faith, Rico continued.

'I think I must have passed out again because when I woke up I remember it was dark and I was being lifted into a barrow. I was convinced they were trash men who thought that I was dead, so they were going to throw me into their lorry to dispose of my body at the municipal tip. After all that was what usually happened to dead street kids.'

'That's awful, kids not even allowed a proper burial,' a shocked Tim interrupted.

'The next thing I remember was lying on a bed with white sheets. The sun was streaming in through the window and everything was so peaceful; I thought I was in heaven! Then I noticed that my head was bandaged and that my ribs were sore every time I breathed, but they too had been bandaged and that my left leg was in a plaster. I could feel a big pad on my stomach and wondered what it was. Just as I was trying to work out where I was, a young woman with a beautiful warm smile came over to me and held my hand. She told me she was Flora and that I was safe. She and her sister, Louise, told me that an old lady had knocked on their door to let them know that there was a boy lying on the street. It was the two sisters who had put me in the barrow to wheel me round to their house. Flora said that one of her other sisters, Ella, was a doctor and she had examined me and realised that I needed surgery so I was taken to the American Hospital straightaway. The surgeon discovered that the beating had damaged one of my internal organs, my spleen, which had to be removed. I had woken up twenty-four hours after the surgery.'

'Wow! That's some story,' Tim exclaimed. 'What happened next? Who were the sisters? Were they nuns?'

'No they were three sisters from New York; they believed that God had called them to Iquitos to set up a ministry for street children. Do you remember the bombing of the World Trade Center in New York, when thousands were killed?' Rico asked.

'Oh yes! All too well! I remember watching it as a kid on TV just a few days before we flew to Lima; Dad was about to start his new job in Peru with the Oil Company. The news report showing footage of the planes flying into the twin towers will remain with me for ever, I think.'

'Louise and Flora worked as communications specialists in the south tower; the oldest, Ella, was at medical school in Washington. Miraculously, Louise and Flora were the only ones to escape from their floor of the tower; they lost many good friends that day.'

'Wow, they were so fortunate to survive!' Tim commented. 'But what was the Peruvian connection?'

'Their father, a pastor in a church in upstate New York, had brought his family to Peru long before the 9/11 atrocity. While here all the girls had helped at some street kids' hostel. The sisters decided to use the compensation money they received to start a project for abandoned street children in Iquitos; Ella by then a qualified doctor opted to join them,' Rico said, as he revealed even more of his remarkable story.

'That's just amazing. Something good, came out of something so awful. So what happened to you after that?' Tim asked, desperate to hear the rest of Rico's tale.

'They looked after me and I joined the other twenty-five children in their home for abandoned boys. Once I was healthy again I started to go to school. There I discovered that I was quite smart. Soon I could read and write; I became quite a 'whizz' kid at maths too,' Rico explained rather proudly.

'When did you change your name to Federico?' Tim enquired, somewhat confused.

'That was Flora's idea. You see I didn't have any papers: no birth certificate, no social security card so they couldn't get any state health care for me. As far as the government was concerned I didn't exist. I didn't even know my last name or my birthday so Flora said that they would have to get papers for me. So I was named Federico Manuel De Seville as that sounded very impressive and they hoped the authorities would accept this. The sisters started calling me Federico as a bit of a joke and finally it stuck,' Rico replied with a smile.

'Why nursing?' Tim asked.

'You were right, God loves even street boys; He certainly saved this one. I was sure I was going to be dumped into the rubbish truck that night and I remember feeling relieved because my suffering in this world would be over. I decided that since God had been good and answered my prayer, that night as I lay in the gutter, then I should try and help others,' Rico replied, humbly. 'I did well enough in my exams to go to the college to study nursing. I didn't want to stay in the city so when I heard about the post in the jungle town of Intuto, I applied.

'What were the chances that you and I would meet again and in this way?' Tim asked, still shocked by all he had just heard.

'What about this tribe? They seem to be very suspicious of you. Do you think they will help us or will they hand us over to the Baron?' Rico asked, changing the subject completely.

'Maybe they've had a bad experience of gringos before. Nothing to do with the Baron,' Tim suggested. 'I don't fancy our chances of escaping from here but if they wanted to kill us, I don't think they would have provided food for us. What do you think?'

'Like you. We mustn't give them the excuse to kill us. If we do make it past the guards to the jungle we might be lost for weeks and we have to try and rescue your friend Rick. You said that the deadline for the ransom was coming up soon,' Rico cautioned.

'Your right, Rick's life is in danger too. On balance, we get some sleep and pray that the chief chooses to help us,' Tim concluded.

Chapter 15

Ancient Beliefs

The boys were well looked after which encouraged both of them. Breakfast was followed by a trip down to the river for a swim and a wash. By now, Tim had a very untidy beard which he wished he could remove; it was itchy and uncomfortable in the sauna-like heat. Their guards were always with them but never threatened them in any way. While down at the river Tim noticed that there were lookouts posted on several vantage points around the village. He thought this was unusual and passed comment to Rico.

'They're a bit nervous aren't they?' Rico said. 'I don't think it has anything to do with us either.'

'Do you think they've been attacked by another tribe?' Tim suggested.

'Maybe, I've heard that there are some rivalries among the tribes that go back many generations, but I was told these groups lived deeper in the jungle near the Ecuador border,' Rico replied, as he watched a few of the young men prepare arrows in the shade of a palm tree.

Tim and Rico were escorted back to their hut but allowed to lie in the hammocks on the veranda. This allowed them to watch the activities of the community. Tim noted there were very few teenage girls around; perhaps they were out in the fields he thought to himself. The older women seemed very subdued sitting around in huddles of threes and fours chewing yuca roots for the local 'hooch'.

'They really like their masato, don't they?' Tim commented, as he observed the women spit the yuca juice into the fermentation pot.

'Yeah every village has several vats on the go at any one time. There's a lot of alcohol in it you know,' Rico said, with a twinkle in his eye.

'Oh yes! Had a few too many have you?' Tim teased his friend.

'Each village shows hospitality by offering their brew. When I first started visiting the outlying villages here in Intuto region, I felt I had to take some but I found out it was really strong. Now I say that, because I'm on official business from the Ministry of Health, I'm not allowed to drink alcohol. So far it has been accepted and I've not offended the chief but it can be a fine line to follow because if you offend the top man you can be thrown out of the village, which of course means the children don't get their baby jabs,' Rico explained, as he lay in his hammock.

'Quite a difficult position to be in; I guess you'll have to learn how to discreetly pour it behind you, as I often do. It tastes reasonable but it's how it's made that's so disgusting, UGH!!' Tim replied, with a little shiver of revulsion.

The sound of a pecky-pecky engine caught the boy's attention; Tim noticed the lookouts give a friendly wave indicating this canoe was no threat. Others in the village who heard the distinctive sound, checked for the signal, and then ran to the jetty.

'This must be the chief coming back,' Rico suggested, raising himself up to get a better look.

'He must be a popular man considering the welcome he is receiving,' Tim commented. 'Let's hope he's a nice man too!'

Within the hour the two young men were led into the chief's hut. He was seated at the top of the room flanked by two of his warriors. Tim and Rico were instructed to sit cross-legged on the floor in front of him; their guards standing over them. The chief's Spanish was good, much to Tim's relief as he didn't want any misunderstandings. Tim and Rico had concocted a story for their captors which didn't include the Baron.

They decide to say that they were a doctor and nurse from Intuto out answering a distress call to a remote community when they'd taken a wrong tributary and become lost. As darkness fell they didn't see the log and so were catapulted into the river; lucky to survive they were making their way back to Intuto. The boys said how grateful they were that the chief's men had found them.

Tim assessed the chief to be in his late thirties, although it was very hard to tell with the native Indians; their skin always looked much older due to the continual exposure to ultraviolet light. The atmosphere was tense. The villagers who had gathered at the back of the hut were silent, even the many children said nothing. Tim could feel his heart rate rising as the chief glared first at him and then at Rico. Everyone in the building was waiting for the chief's response.

'I think you're lying; you're not a doctor! The only strangers around here are from the gold mine and they've stolen eleven of our young women. A month ago they came in broad daylight, when our young men were out hunting. They threatened those that remained in the village with submachine guns and then rounded up our girls. My beautiful daughter is among the captives. You're not a doctor, you're one of those child stealers!'

The shaman, covered in all his fearsome regalia, sprang into action. He whirled around the two captives, spitting at their feet in a mark of utter contempt. The previously silent audience followed his lead and started wailing in a demented drone that sent a chill down Tim's spine. They were in trouble, deep, deep trouble.

'Tomorrow you'll die. My men will take you at first light to the big falls. We'll sacrifice you to Mother Earth and appease her and then we'll get our children back,' the chief pronounced.

The guards dragged the two men to their feet and returned them to their hut, throwing them roughly onto the mud floor before bolting the door securely. The boys lay there for a moment stunned by what had occurred. They could hear the villagers continuing to wail in the distance.

'What now, Rico?' Tim asked. 'Will they do it?'

'Oh yes! They'll do it. These people have ancient beliefs. The witch doctor still holds the tribe under his control. This community has been traumatised by the kidnapping of their young women so the shaman will want to appease Mother Earth with someone, usually a child, as was the ancient custom. We've arrived at a very convenient time for him, and of course the villagers will be happy because he hasn't picked out one of their children,' Rico explained, looking very worried.

'I've heard of child sacrifices in the south of Peru but I didn't know it was still going on up here. I thought such awful deeds ended with the Incas but I've heard recent reports of children being killed in this way,' Tim acknowledged, despondently.

'Yes, I've heard that in these southern communities there's an atmosphere of secrecy and suspicion. If disappearances are reported the authorities do treat such cases as murder, but no one will testify against the perpetrators,' Rico replied.

'When I was in Lima I heard stories of parents who had sent their intelligent, good looking, teenage girls away from towns in the south, to live with relatives in the city; such was the fear that their child would be picked out by the shaman. Apparently those involved in this witchcraft always look for the most beautiful and intelligent of girls; nothing but the best for Mother Earth!' Tim said, shuddering at the thought.

'Why is it always children who are victimised and treated so badly?' Rico questioned. 'Look how we had to live as street children. We had to steal food to survive, all the time at risk of being beaten up by shopkeepers or their hired guards. Remember Andres, he was like a brother to me; he was beaten up so badly that day that he died in the stinking sewer. We knew it was wrong to steal but what do you do when you and your friends are starving? Worse still, boys could earn a few coins to buy food if they allowed themselves to be abused by perverts for their sick, sexual pleasures. What sorts of adults do that?'

Tim could see Rico was suffering a flashback to his life on the streets, probably back with Andres the night he died. The young nurse was lying on his back in the dirt with his hands over his eyes, quietly sobbing for his close friend.

'Rico, it's alright we'll get out of here I promise you,'

Tim said full of confidence. 'This is pure evil we are up against; God is not going to let us down. Do you trust God, Rico?' Tim said as he put his arm around his friend, who was clearly distraught.

'Yes I do, but He seems a long way off just now,' Rico replied, wiping away his tears.

'Right! How are we going to get out of here?' Tim asked, trying to shake Rico out of his obvious anguish.

'I don't know. There're even more guards out there now,' Rico said. 'Look there's two at the door and another two out here at the back!'

He had just finished speaking when the wailing from the villagers grew louder and louder. Peering through the slats the boys could see the shaman leading the entire village in the direction of their hut. The witch doctor danced furiously at the head of the train of frenzied people. Soon they were only twenty metres from the prison. Tim was convinced they were going to be lynched there and then.

Suddenly a great drumbeat began to sound; it stopped the villagers in their tracks. The lookout on the opposite bank of the river was sounding the alarm: the men folk ran for their weapons, the women and kids took off into the jungle.

It turned out to be a false alarm. Tim and Rico watched as five warriors and their families, from a different tribe, left their canoes and clambered up the steep bank from the river. Although heavily armed they posed no threat to the village; they came with gifts. The two men were relieved that their captors, now distracted, were much calmer and keen to sit down with their visitors to hear their news. The women were recalled and soon the cooking pots were on. The guests were going to be treated to a jungle banquet.

'We need to find a way out of here tonight!' Tim said. 'We can't risk trying to break out in the morning.'

'Yes, I agree. But have you any ideas?' Rico asked, as he paced around the room looking for any obvious escape routes.

'No, but let's hope they get drunk tonight. That's our best chance,' Tim concluded thoughtfully.

'If we can make it to the river we can jump in one of the visitors' canoes and head downstream; we're bound to come to Intuto,' Rico suggested, feeling a bit more positive now.

'Yeah but how do we get out of here? We've no tools. Do you think they'll feed us tonight? Last supper and all that,' Tim asked. 'We could always "jump" them then and make a run for it.'

'What do you mean "the last supper"?' Rico asked, confused.

'In the UK a condemned man, before his execution, would always get to choose his last meal but we don't have capital punishment anymore so it doesn't happen now,' Tim clarified.

'We might be able to force a piece of wood here,' Rico suggested. 'But it'll make a lot of noise; let's hope they start singing again soon.'

'What about going through the roof? If I lift you up on my shoulders, could you grasp the beam and pull yourself up? Then you could help me up,' Tim said, his arms stretched above his head to estimate the height of the beam.

'That might work but we'll have to wait until much later before we make any attempt at escape. If they're sober someone is bound to spot us,' Rico said.

The two friends settled down to wait. Darkness fell and

the village began to 'party' as was the custom when visitors arrived. The noise from the assembled villagers sitting around the campfire grew louder as more and more masato was consumed. Out came the drums and the dancing started, the young and old whirling around the big central fire. Rico checked the guards and spotted that there were only two at the door now; the others must have gone off to join in the festivities. Supper didn't materialise but the boys weren't interested in food anyway.

As the evening wore on into the night the women and children left for bed leaving the young men, still imbibing heavily, seated in small huddles around the fire; some looked as if they had fallen asleep.

Tim and Rico decided it was about time to make their escape. Just as Rico had climbed onto Tim's shoulders they were startled by a noise at the door as the bolt was moved; in slipped two young warriors. Tim and Rico thought they had been caught 'red handed' trying to escape but no, the warriors signalled to Tim and Rico to keep quiet. Tim lowered his friend to the ground both now in a state of bewilderment. The taller of the two hunters smiled reassuringly before pulling a small wooden cross from under his torn shirt; the other lifted the oar he was carrying. Quickly the warriors signalled to Tim and Rico to follow them. Stunned, Tim and Rico realised they had no option but to trust the hunters and so went with them into the night.

Once in the forest the group made their way to the river where a third hunter was waiting for them with a canoe equipped with a peck–pecky. Once everyone was in the vessel, each paddled like fury until about half an hour later it was safe to start the engine. The canoe hugged the riverbank to give them as much camouflage as possible so they wouldn't be spotted by any of the Baron's men. Soon the small tributary joined a much bigger river which Tim believed was the Tigre but communication with the warriors was impossible as they spoke a strange dialect. Tim hoped that when they arrived in Intuto someone would be able to translate for him.

Half an hour later, as they joined yet another river, Tim realised just how lost he and Rico had been! Close to dawn the little canoe was approaching Intuto; the silhouette of the township could just be made out in the moonlight. But suddenly, Tim had a horrible thought: what if the Baron's men were waiting for them?

Chapter 16

Published

Katie was so excited by the outcome of the afternoon that she was back in her flat before she remembered she was meeting a colleague, after work, for coffee. It was five thirty; hopefully some of the other guys from the office had gone too. Katie reached for her mobile phone but found a text waiting for her. It was from Laura! Just before they had parted that sunny afternoon, Laura had asked for Katie's mobile number but the journalist didn't think she would ever hear from Laura again.

The message read 'In my new country, at my new home, starting my new life. Any progress? Laura.'

Katie quickly texted back, 'Good to hear your news. Hopefully going out in a Sunday magazine, next week! Katie.'

A quick phone call to her new office-mates to apologise and the working day was over. But not for this girl, as soon as Sandra sent through the draft there would be more to do, Katie thought, but first she must email her parents, before they went to bed, to let them know what was going on.

Her supper was almost finished when the phone rang;

the screen indicated an international call. Would it be Tim in Peru or her parents in India? she wondered.

'Hi Mum, how are you? I know it's really exciting. Imagine a 'rookie' like me being published in the *Sunday Tribune*! It might all be a mistake and the *Tribune* editor will change his mind,' Katie declared, her confidence fleeing again.

'I know I'm always doing myself down, but you have to admit it's quite a surprise. I know it's a shocking story and one that definitely needs to be told, but I didn't think it would go any further than *The Herald*! So I can't join you in London for another two weeks at the earliest, but it's for a good cause. The girl, Laura, sent me a text so she obviously wants to keep in touch, which is good.'

'Sorry Mum, ... I didn't catch that. ... No, I haven't heard from Tim. ... I wasn't expecting to, he's still in the jungle isn't he? ... He's not coming back to London just now. I thought he was going to 'Aus' at the end of his Peru visit. ... Don't worry Mum he'll be fine,' Katie stated, a little surprised by her mother's obvious anxiety.

'He's up in Nueva Casa for eight weeks or more remember. This is only the end of his fifth week. ... How's he supposed to communicate anyway? ... Oh Mum, stop worrying he's a man now and perfectly capable of looking after himself. What's more Miguel and Ronaldo will watch out for him. ... I'll have to go Mum. Is Dad OK?' Katie said, as she leaned over to put the kettle on for a cuppa.

'When are you due into London? ... Sunday evening, great speak to you again then. Have a safe trip. ... Love you. Bye,' Katie said, trying to reassure her mother but she realised that her mother was worried about Tim for some reason.

Saturday lunchtime and still no email from Sandra! Katie was getting exasperated with her boss as she had a very busy Sunday planned. The student played the flute in the Praise Band and this Sunday she was involved in the morning service and an evening concert in an old folk's residence.

She needn't have worried as by early afternoon the piece was in her inbox. With a certain amount of fear and trepidation the trainee journalist opened up the email. To her surprise there was a covering note in very friendly tones; not something she had experienced from Sandra before as she had always made it clear who was the boss. Opening up the draft was a pleasant surprise too: the comments were all very constructive. All things the student felt she could correct easily; except for one piece!

Sandra asked for a fuller explanation of Laura's failure to tell her mother what had been going on, especially after the abuse by the 'cousins'. Katie re-read her article; she thought she had covered this fairly well.

The young journalist sat back and tried to imagine herself in Laura's position. Throughout her ordeal the victim had to deal with two powerful emotions: firstly love then fear. Katie could see that Laura was a shy girl, who was slightly overweight and that she had quite bad acne; two problems that could lead to low self-esteem. This Wayne 'beast' must have deliberately targeted this young nervous, spotty teenager as she would be easy to entrap with flattery and gifts. Laura fell for his deception; she genuinely thought she loved him and that he loved her.

Katie reckoned that Wayne probably bragged to his 'cousins' that Laura would be 'his' in a very short time; initially his 'noose' lay gently over her shoulders ready for the next stage. He knew that as soon as his 'cousins' abused her, Laura would try to run, but compromising photographs and threats to her sister would keep her under control. The noose would tighten, and then fear would be the emotion in charge.

Now Katie could see clearly how Wayne and others like him operated. Laura was his cash crop, nothing more than a commodity, a body to sell as often as he could find customers. All premeditated before he had even met Laura, she was the unfortunate victim. How many other victims are out there? Katie wondered. How many other people like Wayne? Katie shuddered as she thought of the disgusting money-making crime that was occurring in her nation. After her internet research she knew it was happening in just about every country of the world!

Quickly she put her thoughts into the document and attended to the other corrections. She decided it would be best to delay sending it off to Sandra until the morning as with fresh eyes she would eliminate any typos.

Sunday was a good day for Katie. Up early, she checked over her feature article, zapped it off to Sandra and then went off to church for a band practice before the service. She was so busy she didn't even have time to dwell on her work; it was just what she needed. Luke, one of the young guitarists, invited Katie to join him and some others from the church for lunch, followed by a walk along the canal. Luke was an English teacher in the local secondary school and he and Katie had been getting along rather well recently, she thought, so she readily accepted the invitation.

The sun shone, the birds sang and the group of eight had a brilliant afternoon together, before going off in the early evening to the residential home. By the time Katie's head hit the pillow she was happily exhausted. Instead of thinking about dangerous predators, Katie fell asleep thinking that she and Luke were growing closer.

———※———

The next two days at work went by in a flash; Sandra was great. She included Katie in everything to do with the submission to the *Tribune*. Bob the photographer invited Katie to the photo-shoot and was very keen for her opinion. Bob set up the picture as previously discussed in Sandra's office: a dark-haired female model sitting on a chair staring out through a third floor window. Katie's suggestion to dirty the windows a little and have a rip in the model's blouse around the shoulder was accepted. The black and white image was dramatic; Sandra was impressed when she saw it.

By Wednesday four o'clock, and much to Katie's relief, the *Tribune*'s editor, Graham, had acknowledged receipt of the article and photographs. Just before six in the evening, as Katie was going through the supermarket checkout, Sandra phoned.

'Well done young lady. On time and accepted by the editor of the *London Tribune*; that's quite an achievement for a student!' Sandra said, congratulating Katie. 'All we have to do is wait and see how the article is received by the public on Sunday.'

'Thanks Sandra, that's wonderful. Bye.' Katie said, lost for words.

'Hey! Have you just won the lottery?' the checkout girl exclaimed. 'I haven't seen anyone with a grin as big as yours today and I started at eight o'clock this morning!'

'No, just some very good news. Thanks,' Katie said, as she lifted her shopping and dashed for the exit. Luke and some of Katie's friends from church were picking her up at seven o'clock so she needed to get a move on; they were heading out to the cinema. Now that everything had been sent to the *Tribune* she was relaxed and looking forward to the evening, but she still had to decide what to wear!

The next few days at work went very quickly. Katie's colleagues seemed to be genuinely excited for her as they all accepted it was quite a scoop the youngster had made and brilliant for her future career.

'You've written an excellent piece of work. Lots of good detail,' Alf remarked, when he came over to Katie's desk. The student knew that was praise indeed, the senior journalist at the paper was not known for his compliments!

'You might make a good journalist someday, Katie,' John teased.

'Thanks John. I was just fortunate; in the right place at the right time,' she replied, modestly.

Katie was quite shocked at her own reply because she knew in her heart that coming across Laura's story was no accident. This encounter had nudged her down a path unfamiliar to her, one she hadn't even realised existed until a week ago – the murky, darkness of trafficking. In the cathedral she promised God she would do everything she could to stop this terrible abuse of young girls.

Sunday morning, Katie's alarm was set for six o'clock. She was determined she was going to buy the *Tribune* and see the article herself before any friends or family were even up. She tumbled out of bed, dressed and dived downstairs to the local newsagent, which was only a hundred metres from her home. The papers had just arrived, thrown off in their bundles from the delivery van.

'You'll have to wait love. I'm just on my own today, the paperboy's off sick again,' the newsagent declared, obviously in a bad mood.

'No hurry. It's the *Tribune* I'm after,' she explained, leaning against the shop counter patiently.

Katie decided to wander round the convenience store picking up some morning rolls on the way. She liked this shop as it had almost everything in it and it was open from very early to very late. She knew the owners worked incredibly hard so she liked to support them when she could, but on her meagre student income, most of the time, she used the superstore across the river.

'Here you are lass,' the newsagent called, as he cut through the tight plastic tape around the paper bundle.

Quickly paying for her purchases Katie ran home; she ripped open the plastic wrapping of the Sunday broadsheet and searched through the multiple enclosures for the magazine.

She couldn't believe her eyes! The front cover photograph was the one Bob had taken on the photo shoot – the girl with torn blouse looking out through the window! Katie was stunned. Nervously she opened the magazine to find the article; it was halfway through and laid out so well. The young journalist excitedly read the entire piece; they hadn't missed out anything or had they? Laura's story was fully explained but Katie's disgust at the authorities and their failure to believe Laura's mother, that her daughter had been abducted was toned down considerably. Perhaps the *Tribune* didn't want to upset the 'powers that be' or perhaps Katie had been a bit too critical considering she only had one side of the story.

As Katie looked through the Sunday magazine she came across the article that Sandra had mentioned about trafficking from Eastern Europe. Again the photographs were in black and white to give the reader the sense of injustice and blackness associated with the topic. She threw the open magazine onto the kitchen table while she made herself some coffee. The photograph in the trafficking article caught Katie's attention: most of a girl's face was deliberately hidden by a scarf but the eyes of the young woman stared across the table at Katie, as she sipped her drink. The dark, sunken eyes were just like Laura's: they told of shock, trauma, and the hopelessness of a brutalised young woman.

It took Katie ten minutes to read the piece, by the end tears were streaming down her face. The victim this time was Katerina, again not her real name. She had fallen in love with a boy, Demian, in her native Ukraine. He had invited her to go on a picnic with him and some of his friends to a nearby lake. There, Katerina was drugged and bundled into a car and driven for hundreds of miles to a very remote part of the country where she was kept captive, with ten other girls, in an old farm house. There they were sexually assaulted, and beaten by a gang of older men. One girl tried to escape; she was beaten senseless by one of the cruellest men Katerina had ever met. The girl died the next day, she was only fifteen. After two weeks they were loaded onto a bus and driven to Paris, by now the girls knew what to expect if they tried to escape. In Paris they were divided up into pairs and dropped off at different addresses in the middle of the night. Katerina found herself in a brothel close to the Eiffel tower: she could glimpse the iconic building from her room window.

For two years Katerina was held in the same room, servicing men from all over the world. She was not allowed to leave the building; she was a prisoner. If she complained she was beaten. The young woman felt defiled and hopeless.

One night a client arrived who was different from the others. He didn't want to use her; he just wanted to talk. His name was Françoise, initially Katerina was very reluctant to speak to him, and she didn't want to tell him anything in case he was part of the trafficking gang. Over the next month Françoise kept coming back to Katerina but each time it was only to speak to her. The young Ukrainian told him a little about herself, where she was from, about her family but when he asked her if she was happy working there she lied and told him that she was; she was so scared! Françoise told her about trafficking, about her rights there in Paris and asked if he could help her. But Katerina was too frightened; she had seen what had happened to other girls who had tried to escape.

One day, as Katerina was trying to catch a little sleep, she could hear the sobs of Jessica, a Romanian girl, in the room next door; she had arrived a few weeks earlier. The girl seemed to cry all night; Katerina resolved that if Françoise came back again she would ask him for help. She couldn't live in this hell any more, death would be preferable she thought and maybe he would help Jessica next door too.

The following week Françoise did return and he asked Katerina again if he could help her; this time she agreed. He was an undercover policeman, passionate about human rights, who worked in the fight against organised international crime. All he asked of her was to give evidence against her captors; he would make sure she was given a new identity. But Katerina was still very frightened for her family as the traffickers had threatened to attack them should she go to the police; she knew how violent they could be. Françoise promised that she would be able to give evidence behind a screen and with her voice disguised so the criminals wouldn't know who had testified against them. The policeman, having gained Katerina's trust explained that he was part of a big operation and that very shortly there would be action taken on a large scale across Paris. Katerina didn't understand what he meant until ten days later, at four in the morning, the Parisian police forced their way into the brothel where Katerina was held captive. Françoise rescued Katerina and the other girls; they were taken to a safe house where they were looked after and given medical attention.

Katerina did give evidence in court and some prosecutions were made but sadly none of the traffickers were caught.

Katie was numbed by what she had just read. If this article was to be believed then the abuse of young women was widespread and highly organised. Her mobile rang interrupting Katie's ruminations.

'Hi Luke. You're up early. ... Yes, I have a copy; I'm very pleased. The paper has presented it well. ... Did you see the photo on the front page? That's ours. Isn't that amazing? ... Have you read the other article, entitled "Trafficked"? ... It's a real shocker too.'

'... Yes that's the one: the girl with the dark eyes. Have a read and we can chat about it after church. ... Oh, that's great I'd hoped you would be able to come tonight. Gina, Sally, Nick and Josh are all coming, so we should have a good get together. ... Bye, see you later,' Katie said, excitedly.

She had just hung up when her Mum phoned; her parents were now safely back home in London. Katie was so looking forward to going up to see them. Soon afterwards her friends Gina and Mark rang. But the next call really surprised her since it was still only eight o'clock on a Sunday morning. It was Sandra.

'... How does it feel to be published by a Sunday paper, you ask? Excited, happy, anxious, a real mixed bag of emotions. ... Thank you for all your help, guidance and encouragement, Sandra. ... Yes, I've read the "Trafficking" article. ... I can hardly believe this is going on. ... Thanks, Sandra, I'll see you tomorrow. Bye'.

A few minutes later Katie received a text message from Laura asking if the article had been published and if she could have a copy. Katie thought for a minute and decided that as the story was now in the public domain she could email the piece to Laura; she would eventually receive a copy from a relative or friend anyway. Within a few minutes Katie sent the article off to Laura wherever she was in the world.

Chapter 17

Help Needed

With Rico's help and much gesticulation they headed for Nueva Casa, by-passing Intuto. Miguel would know how best to help them now, but they would have to be careful because the Baron's men might have Nueva Casa in their sights too. Tim directed the paddlers away from the usual village pontoon at the front, to a little landing area on the banks of the small river that formed the eastern boundary of the community. From here they could scramble up the banking and enter the village from the jungle side and so reach Miguel's hut unnoticed.

The warriors picked up Tim's obvious anxiety and so with machetes unsheathed they followed him to the back of Miguel's house. Tim peered through a gap in the rear wall to see his friend bound, gagged and tied to the centre post of the building. There were two armed men in the hut; one looked to be asleep just inside the doorway facing Miguel, the other was awake sitting on the veranda look-ing out onto the village. Tim was so relieved that he had advised entering the village by the 'back door' otherwise they would have walked straight into the trap. 'Thank you Lord,' he whispered with utter gratitude.

Tim signalled to Rico and the warriors the location of the Baron's men. The warriors exchanged glances and disappeared into the night. Tim was confused, he wondered what was going to happen next. Had their new 'friends' decided to abandon them when they saw the weapons? Were he and Rico going to have to free Miguel on their own? All these disturbing thoughts ran around Tim's mind, but suddenly and simultaneously the gunmen fell face down on the floor. The warriors with clubs in hand stood gleefully over them!

Quickly Tim and Rico joined the others and released the chief. Miguel had been badly beaten by his captors but he still managed a smile.

'Am I glad to see you Tim,' Miguel said, hugging his friend. 'These men have been waiting for you since yesterday; I think they had every intention of shooting you on sight. Just as well you came in the back way.'

'How many more are there?' Tim asked, still feeling very uneasy.

'I think there's another one down at the canoes,' Miguel replied. 'What happened to you? Where did you find these warriors, Tim?'

'It's a long story. Can you speak their dialect?' Tim asked, desperately hoping to improve communication among his new band of friends.

Miguel tried addressing the warriors in Arawan, an ancient language, fortunately they understood. For the next couple of minutes the chief explained to his rescuers what had happened and the location of the remaining fighter. The warriors prepared to depart into the moonless night to neutralise the last of the Baron's men.

'Ask them if they want one of these rifles?' Rico said to

Miguel, trying to be helpful and offer the warriors some extra protection.

The warriors turned and grinned, lifting their machetes! Within ten minutes they returned with a very dazed and disarmed terrorist. They had found a long length of rope on the boat so quickly set about tying up the Baron's men before they regained consciousness.

'Who are your friends, Tim?' Miguel asked again as he watched the tribesmen secure his assailants.

'They're hunters from a village north of Intuto. Some of the young women from their tribe have been kidnapped too and taken to the gold mine where I was held. The chief decided he was going to appease Mother Earth by sacrificing us, but these brave guys rescued us. Maybe you could ask them why they helped us,' Tim suggested.

Miguel spoke with the warriors for several minutes to try and discover their motives for rescuing Tim and Rico. The chief learned that they were close friends who had grown up together. He discovered that the hunters had believed Tim's story, that he was a gringo doctor because his hands were so soft.

The tribesmen had met an American doctor in Intuto two years earlier. Then, Gigo, the oldest of the warriors, had terrible belly-ache and couldn't keep his food in his stomach; he was so ill he thought he was going to die. His friends, Roto and Dide, had heard about the missionary boat that was visiting Intuto so they carried their friend into a canoe and took him downstream to the medical vessel. They were welcomed by Dr Tom, one of the medics on board, who examined Gigo and told him that he needed an operation to remove a rotten piece of his gut. Gigo had related how kind Dr Tom had been and how gentle the gringo nurses were who looked after him. He stayed in their care for almost a week.

The young Indian had tried to understand why these gringos had come to the rainforest; what motivated them to come and help a people they didn't know? he had wondered. One of the young nurses spoke to him about God's love for everyone and explained that it was because of that love she, and the others onboard, wanted to come and work with the villagers here in the Amazon; the medics knew the tribespeople had very little access to health care. They hadn't come to convert them to a new religion but to care for them. But Gigo had never heard of a loving God and wanted to know more about Him.

In addition, Miguel discovered that Gigo's and his friends' sisters were among the girls taken off to the mine and they were very angry and upset by this. The warriors knew that the shaman in their village had been trying to persuade their chief to sacrifice to Mother Earth, to appease her, before some other catastrophe hit the community. Tim and Rico had arrived at the village at the worst possible time. But the three friends decided they couldn't stand by and see innocent men die because of ancient superstitions.

Miguel knew the warriors could not return to their village after they had openly defied their chief so he invited them to live in Nueva Casa, to make it their new home.

'Miguel, have you met Federico before?' Tim enquired of his friend with a smile.

'You are the new nurse at the clinic, aren't you? How did you get involved with all this?' Miguel asked, with a puzzled look.

'Yes, I am. It's an interesting story, I hardly believe it myself,' Rico replied, scratching his head.

'Miguel, do you recall when Katie and I were rescued by street boys in Iquitos? Do you remember we searched for weeks for Rico? This is Rico. He survived after all; he was rescued from the streets by three sisters from the States,' Tim explained.

'That's amazing! You must tell me the whole story when this is over,' Miguel answered, 'but, we have much to do now.'

'Where's Ronaldo? Is he alright?' Tim asked, suddenly remembering about his friend.

'He had to return to Iquitos; we received a message over the radio that his wife was sick. He left this morning by canoe for the village of Berlin. The riverboat has been refloated and is returning to Iquitos the day after tomorrow,' Miguel explained.

'Thank goodness he wasn't in Berlin a couple of days ago when some of those terrorists paid the town a visit.'

'Tim who kidnapped you and why? Where did they take you?' Miguel asked, still unclear as to what was really going on.

As quickly and accurately as possible, Tim gave an account of all that had happened in the days since his abduction. They discussed the imminent danger to Rick's life and of course the terrible circumstances of the trafficked village girls.

'Do you think the army would help us?' Tim queried, recognising that they had very little chance on their own of achieving Rick's freedom, let alone releasing the captive girls.

'I think they would, but you would need to be able to lead them to the mine. Can you do that?' Miguel asked, aware that his friend had only a sparse knowledge of the area and had spent most of his trip to the site in the bottom of a boat.

'I don't think I could. What about you Rico?' Tim asked. 'I suppose not, because we hit that log only about halfway, I'd reckon.'

'I know roughly the direction, but I wouldn't be any help to a patrol,' Rico replied. 'What about Gigo?'

Miguel chatted with Gigo and discovered that he knew exactly where the mine was. The chief had considered attacking the compound to rescue their girls but there were too many heavily armed fighters. The house where the girls were held was constantly guarded. The warriors knew they would be cut to pieces and the womenfolk would be caught in the crossfire. The chief came to Intuto only yesterday to speak with the authorities and asked for help, but the army commander didn't believe there was a gold mine in the region and he decided that the chief wanted military help to sort out some inter-tribal dispute.

'It could be that the commander knows all about the mine and is getting a nice little "back-hander" from the Baron,' Miguel suggested, a scenario that had escaped Tim completely.

'Maybe. But what about the attack on the terrorist's boat, after they kidnapped me?' Tim queried, quite confused.

'Yeah, but you were very near Intuto, not near the mine. The trigger happy soldiers would know nothing of the mine,' Miguel pointed out.

'So what you're saying is that we might be handed back to the Baron or be "accidently taken out" if we go anywhere near the unit commander in Intuto,' Tim replied, incredulously.

'It's a possibility we have to consider. I reckon there are about twenty men in the unit in Intuto, enough to man two high-speed ribs. According to Gigo that would be no match against the Baron's men anyway,' Miguel cautioned. 'I'm not sure of the best way forward.'

'We mustn't forget Rick. I think they'll kill him if no ransom is paid and the due date is the end of the month; only a few days from now,' Tim said, pacing around the hut with frustration.

'I don't think they'll kill him, at least not yet, he's too valuable to them. You on the other hand know where the mine is and if they or their friends find you ...' Miguel cautioned. 'I think we need to get you back to Iquitos and then Lima as soon as possible. These Black Vultures have a long reach.'

'You've got to be kidding. I can't just leave Rick or these young girls as sex slaves and pretend I know nothing about them! Gigo and his friends have risked their lives for Rico and me. We would have been thrown off the top of the waterfall by now if it wasn't for these guys,' Tim argued, really getting himself worked up.

'This isn't a game Tim! People are going to get hurt. This whole village is at risk now that we are holding three of their fighters, not to mention what'll happen to Gigo's village if the Baron finds out they've helped you. These two communities: men, women and kids will be gone. These terrorists are utterly ruthless; Peru has seen it all before with The Shining Path. Tim this is not your fight. I asked you to come to use your medical skills to help my people; now your life is in danger and it's my duty to return you safely home,' Miguel said, as he tried to reason with the young medic.

'That's as maybe, but if we don't make some decisions soon none of us will be around to meet the next riverboat anyway. These guys will have to radio back to base soon and when no one does, the Baron's men will be all over this place like ants looking for them. We need a plan and quickly. What if we contact the American Embassy and let them know about Rick? They'll put pressure on the Peruvian army to rescue him and to do that they'll send a strong enough fighting force with senior commanders,' Tim suggested, a plan beginning to formulate in his mind.

'That's sounds good but how do we get in touch with the American Embassy?' Miguel enquired with a tone of sarcasm.

'We can use the radio here in Nueva Casa can't we? We can get a message to Gilberto in Iquitos this morning. He'll do the rest,' Tim decided with his usual assertiveness. 'You can bet that American intelligence agencies know that Rick was kidnapped but they can't know where he is or they would have rescued him by now.'

'Who's Gilberto?' Rico asked, trying to keep up with Tim's strategic thinking.

'You remember, he's the man who brought soup and bread to the street boys; he still lives in Iquitos,' Tim clarified.

The mood lifted in the chief's hut as the young men discussed at length their plans remembering to keep Gigo and the warriors up to speed.

'Tim, the sun's up now, you and I can go to the radio shack. Gigo and his boys can look after this lot,' Miguel said pointing to the three trussed up fighters. 'Rico you come with us in case we need some more help. Let's hope the Baron's boys don't have to report until later in the morning.'

Tim glanced at his watch as the three made their way to the radio shack; it was ten minutes to six. They managed to raise the Loreto Region Radio Service in Iquitos as soon as the Service was on air; this was a great relief to Miguel as he knew that sometimes, if there were bad electrical storms, contact was impossible. This radio link was the only communication between the remote Amazonian villages and the outside world. The operator in Iquitos promised to phone Gilberto and ask him to come to the radio as soon as he could. All the boys could do was sit and wait.

While they were waiting, Rico told Miguel something of his life as a street boy in Iquitos. The young nurse was about to speak about his rescue from the slums when the radio came to life; it was Gilberto. Miguel, whose Spanish was superior to Tim's and therefore easier to understand over a crackly radio, did all the talking. Gilberto agreed to contact the American embassy in Lima as soon as possible. But Tim wasn't happy with this arrangement.

'Wait, Gilberto!' Tim said, grabbing the microphone. 'We must act quicker than this. Someone might be listening to this message for all we know. ... Phone my father, he should be back in Britain by now; you have the number don't you? ... Tell him what's going on and he'll contact the US Embassy in London. ... We'll get a much faster response if we do it this way. ... Make sure they realise that the local commander is probably being bribed by the Baron. We don't want to be rounded up by the local patrol before lunch. ... Radio back as soon as you know anything. ... Thank you my friend.'

'Can we move this radio?' Tim queried, looking at the bulky instrument.

'Yes, but it's very heavy although we should manage to carry it,' Miguel replied, as he tried to get his arms around the transmitter.

'Then let's take it with us. It's the only way we can keep in touch with Gilberto. The more I think about it, we must stay away from Intuto. Either the Baron's men or a potential rogue commander could take us all down. I'm not sure we can stay here either; the terrorists will be all over here by noon if these thugs don't radio back to the mine. I think we'll have to take off into the jungle,' Tim advised, watching for Miguel's response.

'But, what about my people? There are over twenty families in Nueva Casa. The Baron's men will destroy this village and anyone they can find when they realise we have escaped,' Miguel snapped, thinking of the lives of his people.

'What if one of the fighters makes the call to the Baron?' Rico proposed. 'That would buy us some time.'

'And just how are we going to make that happen?' Tim asked, doubtfully.

'Rico might have a good idea,' Miguel said. 'The little guy, the one who was down by the boat, he looks really frightened lying there on the floor. He looks Columbian; I'll bet he's from the city. He's scared stiff of Gigo; it's probably all his feathers and paint. Maybe if we took him and Gigo down to their boat, we could encourage the Columbian to use the radio sensibly. If he does anything suspicious we'll have time to evacuate the village before the Baron's rescue party gets here. We'll split up the terrorists just to make them even more jumpy but leave the Columbian with Gigo and his brothers. Right let's get back to the others.'

Miguel spent the next hour speaking with each family and explained what was happening. They all promised to be ready to escape into the forest if necessary. The women-folk gathered up the few possessions they had: pots, plates, and a few clothes for the children. The men made ready their weapons and gathered up the tools they needed to start a new village. Like many of the tribespeople in the Amazon they were quite used to moving on; often a whole community would leave an area if the hunting deteriorated or the fishing was poor.

Later Miguel and Tim rejoined Gigo and the Colombian. So far there had been no contact from Gilberto in Iquitos which surprised and worried Tim. Miguel began to question the Columbian about the next radio contact. He refused to speak, so Miguel signalled to Gigo. The warrior walked over and unsheathed his machete; that was all it took for complete cooperation from the captive. Tim was relieved even though he knew that neither he nor Miguel would have sanctioned violence. Within the hour the message that all was well and there had been no sign of Tim was sent to the Baron's base. The next contact was not expected until sunset. As far as Tim and Miguel could see, no mistakes had been made or suspicions aroused during the communication, which was a huge relief, and it had bought them at least twelve hours, maybe more.

By noon Tim was anxious to speak to Gilberto again so he persuaded Miguel to try the radio. To their horror they couldn't get it to work; they tried everything they could, but nothing.

'We've had problems with the radio,' Miguel confessed. 'But it has been good for the last couple of weeks; I guess moving it has just finished it off.'

'That's just great! Now what are we going to do?' Tim questioned, throwing his hands up in frustration.

'What about the radio in Intuto?' Rico offered. 'There are two: one in the police station and one in the clinic.'

'Good point, but who's going to go into town to make the call? Me, you, Miguel, it's not safe for any of us to just wander into the town, is it?' Tim said, sullenly.

'What if you head down to Berlin after sunset?' Miguel suggested. 'You'll be there by morning. Rico can go with you and I'll send some of my hunters with you to make sure you get there safely.'

'Gilberto will have got the message through, I know he will. What if Rico and I try to sneak into the clinic after dark?' Tim replied. 'The other alternative is we wait!'

'Yeah! But how long can we keep kidding on the Baron?' Rico said, reminding the others that the Baron wouldn't leave his men here for ever.

'We wait another twenty-four hours. It's too dangerous to send you two to the clinic; they'll be waiting for you there. I'll send my people into the jungle for a few days just in case anything goes wrong but some of the young men will stay with us,' Miguel said, with an authority that even Tim knew he couldn't challenge.

'I think you're right; we have to be here to guide the soldiers to the mine if we're to have any hope of saving Rick or freeing the young captives,' Tim agreed.

Chapter 18

Surprise Visit

The rest of the day passed quickly. The families were loaded into canoes, some to the point of sinking, or so Tim thought, and then they headed up the river from Nueva Casa. It would have been too dangerous to go anywhere near the Rio Tigre.

'How far are they going?' Rico asked, as he watched them leave.

'About a month ago our hunter's found an abandoned village upstream. After an hour they should reach the tributary and then it's about another two hours paddling up the smaller river; they should be there by sunrise,' Miguel replied. 'They'll be well out of harm's way there.'

Miguel organised the remaining men into shifts to guard the village. One man was sent to a vantage point across the river where he would see any vessel coming upstream from Intuto. Should there be any sign of the Baron's men they would be able to escape into the rainforest. Miguel's men knew this part of the forest well now, so they would be able to disappear quickly.

By dusk Tim was shattered. The heat, the lack of sleep and the long walk through the jungle had caught up with him. With Miguel's encouragement he decided to lie in a hammock until it was time for his watch. He tried hard to stay awake by reliving the events of the previous days.

He couldn't get the sight of the young girls, being pawed by older men at the gold mine, out of his mind. Some of the girls looked as if they were as young as twelve or thirteen. To hear that two of them were Gigo's sisters made it even worse although he knew all the girls were somebody's sister or daughter.

Then there was Rick: such a pleasant, quiet man who had been using his particular expertise to help develop a country. He had been badly beaten during his capture but even so he had huge compassion for the Peruvian people. Tim recalled their disturbing conversation about modern-day slavery and he saw the evidence of such barbarism at the Baron's compound. The men at the site had to work seventeen hours a day, mining gold. The brutality meted out by terrorists was shocking: beatings and executions for anyone who tried to escape. Boys, some as young as eight or nine years old had been snatched as well; the lucky ones carried water but some had to go down the dark, frightening mine shafts.

Tim woke to find a hand tightly across his mouth and a knife to his throat! In the half darkness he could see two other figures in the hut. The Baron's men had found him. The Columbian must have used code or something to let his boss know something was up. Tim's heart was pounding in his chest. This was it! He was dead!

'Twitch as much as a muscle and you're gone pal,' the assailant said, in a Texan accent.

One of the others came over and shone a light in Tim's face.

'You must be the young Doc?' the man said. 'Tim isn't it?'

With that Tim was released and allowed to stand up.

'I'm Major Jack Irving of the US Marine Corp. I hear you're looking for some help,' Jack said, as he shook Tim's hand.

'You could say that. You got here really fast,' Tim replied, shocked but relieved.

'We've been in the Amazon region for a while looking for Rick Jefferson. Can't tell you exactly where we've come from but thanks to modern communications we're here now,' the Major replied with a big grin, which exposed his white teeth behind his heavily camouflaged face.

Just at that point Major Irving received a radio message from one of his men.

'… Is the perimeter secure? All buildings checked … OK. Bring the chief over. Good job, Mike.'

'So Tim, you know where they're holding Rick?' the Major asked. 'Can you direct us there? Can you give us details of the location?'

Tim explained all that had happened. He pointed out on the officer's map roughly where the mine was. Tim told him that Gigo, with the help of Miguel, would be able to tell him more accurately about the camp and would be able to take them there.

The American confirmed that other US units were working with the Peruvian army but had been searching for Rick to the south of here, in the Madros area. When word reached the Pentagon that morning, Major Irving and his men, the nearest commando unit, were dispatched to find and protect Tim and his friends. The Peruvian army had been watching the commander in Intuto, Captain

Fernando Garcia de Rusto, for a few months so the news that he might be working with the Baron didn't come as a surprise.

'Captain De Rusto is going to get quite a shock tomorrow when three, fifty-strong platoons of Peruvian commandos show up in his little town. It's fair to say the Peruvian army isn't happy with the Captain, he has allowed the notorious Baron to work without interference on his patch. This incident has the potential to give the Peruvian government a red face. I think he'll be looking at court martial and a long unpleasant stretch in a Peruvian jail,' Irving explained.

'So can you tell us the plan, Major?' Tim asked, impatiently.

'Once the Peruvian marines arrive it's their shout as we're on Peruvian soil, but because it's a US citizen we're trying to rescue, we'll assist.'

'What about the young girls and the boys? Do the commandos know about them?' Tim queried; he was concerned that they might be at risk if there was a big fire-fight.

'Yip! My commanding officer has been briefed by his opposite number in Lima. They've the same information that we have and are very used to this sort of scenario. In fact part of the platoon on its way, has a special section that is highly trained in hostage work. Apparently in the south of Peru, in the Madros region I mentioned earlier, many illegal gold mines have been opened up. You'll know that the price of gold has rocketed around the world due to the economic crisis in the West, so organised gangs want their piece of the action. They've been trafficking young men from poor villages to do much of the hard labour and girls from the city slums to work in the brothels at these camps. The Peruvian government is cracking down hard on these gangs so the army is often involved in freeing these people,' the Major expounded.

'Some of that reached the UK press last year. It's hard to believe one lot of people can treat another group so badly. It's as if these enslaved men and woman are worth nothing,' Tim commented, deeply troubled by what he had just had confirmed.

'On the contrary, these trafficked folks are worth a huge amount! Criminal gangs all over the world have discovered that once a bale of cocaine is used they can make no further money out of it, but give them a human being and they can be used again and again. It might be to mine for gold or make money in a brothel, either way they have lots of value,' Major Irving explained further, surprising Tim with his knowledge.

'Truly shocking, isn't it?' Tim sighed.

'Now you can rest easy. I've thirty marines deployed round this village so get some sleep. We'll talk some more later,' the officer said, as he left to check on his men.

Tim returned to his hammock. Miguel and Rico were now with him and the three men were guarded by two big US marines; fortunately these heavily armed soldiers were there to protect them. More relaxed, but with even more on his mind, Tim couldn't sleep. He hoped he could persuade the Major to allow him to go on the mission but he wasn't sure how he was going to achieve that. He knew that Miguel would have to go because he was the only one who could speak Gigo's dialect. Perhaps he could go along as the medic, maybe Major Jack would buy into that especially as there would be a US citizen to look after.

In the morning the Major returned to talk to Tim and the warriors about the layout of the Baron's hideout. Tim needn't have worried about having to persuade the Major to let him go on the expedition. The young doctor was the only one who knew exactly where in the compound Rick was being held. He was essential to the success of the mission.

The next day passed quickly and without incident. The off watch section of marines enjoyed a swim in the river along with Tim, Miguel and Rico. Everyone felt safe now that the soldiers were there. They had taken the terrorists into their custody too, so that was one less worry. Fortunately the little Columbian had continued to oblige with flawless, regular communications back to their headquarters and as far as they were aware, the terrorist group had no idea what was about to hit them.

Tim noted that Gigo and his brothers kept themselves to themselves and despite knowing that their sisters were about to be rescued seemed very tense. Tim took Miguel to speak to them to find out their concerns.

The conversation with the warriors took sometime but Miguel discovered they were very worried on two counts. Firstly that their sisters might be injured or even killed in the crossfire when the army attacked the compound, but Tim was able to reassure them that the number of Peruvian commandos would easily outnumber the terrorists. Digging deeper Tim realised they had a much more sensitive issue on their minds. Who would look after their sisters when they were returned to their village? The girls were all under fifteen years old and there was no way the brothers could return to protect them. None of the men of their village would want them as wives because they had been in the Baron's brothel. Once Miguel realised the problem he was quick to extend his offer to the warriors to include their sisters too. They could have a fresh start in Nueva Casa; the warriors were delighted with the plan.

Just before dusk, earlier than expected, two Peruvian naval boats came up the river from Intuto. Major Irving was there to meet the Peruvian captain who bounded out of the first rib. After a respectful exchange of salutes the two men shook hands.

'Is everything under control in Intuto, Captain Garcia?' the Major asked his Peruvian colleague.

'Yes sir. Captain De Rusto has been relieved of his command and is now in military custody. I've come to escort you and your men to the town. Are you ready, Sir?'

'Yes. We've six civilians coming with us; five Peruvians and the British doctor. He's the one who was kidnapped by the terrorist group and held at the camp. His knowledge of the precise location of Rick Jefferson is crucial. He has agreed to provide extra medical support if required,' Major Irving replied.

Within five minutes Nueva Casa was deserted. The convoy of six military ribs sped down the short distance to Intuto. The jetty was crowded with naval fast boats. Sentries were everywhere with a machine gun post on the bank overlooking the harbour area. The locals were nowhere to be seen; a curfew had been ordered just in case any of the Baron's men were around. The commandos had systematically searched the town for his men and the community was now sealed off. The army couldn't run the risk of anyone tipping off the Baron; he had been wanted by the police for murder, cocaine smuggling and gun running for over two years.

Half an hour after they arrived there was great commotion down at the jetty. Two more naval boats arrived but this time from the north of Intuto. The Peruvian commandos had captured two terrorists about four kilometres up the Rio Tigre. These two boats had been sent by their young Captain further north to lay a trap for any of the Baron's men who might have taken off into the jungle, when the military arrived in Intuto. The trap had worked a treat.

'I'm most impressed, Captain. The mission would have failed if these two guys had escaped. Well done,' Major Irving said, acknowledging the younger man's success.

'It's all down to experience, Sir. We're beginning to understand a lot more about how this Baron works. We almost had him last year but he was tipped off. When we arrived at his camp the fires weren't even hot, he was long gone. I feel good about this one; we're going to catch him tomorrow. He'll not know what's hit him. Come let's eat and rest, we've an early start,' the Captain said, smiling with confidence.

Tim had overheard their conversation and he too felt quite confident the mission was going to succeed. However he discovered that Miguel was becoming increasingly nervous about the whole operation, so Tim further clarified the plan which reassured the chief, at least a little. Both knew that young men would be killed: some soldiers, some terrorists, possibly even some of the young girls, but they were grateful that there were many highly specialised soldiers around them, so hopefully this would help minimise the casualties.

After supper, all were told to rest until the briefing meeting at midnight.

Chapter 19

Much Concern

By the time her friends arrived that evening Katie was beginning to feel quite exhausted. Her mobile had gone off all day. The inbox on her two email accounts: student and work just kept filling up. The student ones were from friends congratulating her on her success and easy to deal with. But some of the work ones seemed a little daunting and she knew they would be best kept until Monday morning, after she had had a chance to chat to Sandra and get some advice on how to reply to the more awkward ones. Like the one from Detective Inspector Harold Moore of the Serious Crime Squad who wanted to interview her. Or the email from Mr Rupert Duff, the owner of *The Herald*; he wanted to meet with her to congratulate her on her success.

Halfway through the evening the telephone rang; it was Katie's father. She could tell straightaway something was wrong. She had spoken to her mother before breakfast and all had seemed well then.

'Kidnapped! ... Tim kidnapped! When? ... Who by? ... I am calm! ...' Katie screamed at her dad, stamping up and down on the hall carpet.

'You mean he was kidnapped but he's now free and there's an American still being held ... Tim's what? ... Going to lead an army unit back to the terrorist compound! ... Is he mad? How do you know all this?' Katie demanded of her father.

'What's wrong Katie?' Luke asked, anxiously.

'Shhhh! I'll tell you in a minute,' Katie replied as she beckoned to Luke to come and stand beside her.

'... Gilberto, Tim contacted Gilberto so he could relay the message to you ... Is Tim alright?' Katie asked, nervously.

'... Thank goodness! No, I'm not on my own; I have some friends here from the church. ... Oh, Dad I hope he'll be alright. ... How's Mum? She knew something was wrong at the weekend. ... How did she know?' Katie remembered, wondering how her mother had known Tim was in danger.

'I'll ask one of the girls to keep me company tonight. ... Dad, I'll be fine, just promise me you'll keep me informed,' Katie begged her father. 'Bye Dad, speak later.'

Katie stood in stunned silence. Luke put his arm around her shoulder to comfort her; she dropped her head easily onto his shoulder.

'Has Tim been kidnapped?' he asked gently.

'He was but he has escaped; now he's leading an army unit back to the compound to help free an American. That'll be so dangerous,' Katie whimpered, as she buried her head into Luke's shoulder. The pair stood in the hall for a few minutes before returning to the sitting room where Katie shared her news with the rest of her friends.

Gina agreed to spend the night at Katie's flat, which cheered the young reporter up; she didn't want to be on her own, knowing that Tim was in such danger.

The next week was agonising for Katie. She wanted to go home to be with her parents as she knew her mother would be in a terrible state; the news of Tim would open up all the old wounds her mother suffered when she and Tim were lost in the Amazon, but her father wouldn't hear of it. He advised his daughter to stay at work and help the police as best she could with the 'Laura' story.

Once back in the office on the Monday, the young journalist sat at her desk and worked steadily through the emails, answered the telephone calls and other queries that came her way as a result of the publication in the *Sunday Tribune*.

The meeting with *The Herald*'s owner turned out to be very interesting. Sandra and Katie were invited to his Oxford home on the Friday evening. Katie had never visited such a grand country house: a beautiful tree-lined drive, with cattle grazing in fields on either side, led up to a Victorian mansion with an ornate stairway leading to the front door. Sandra saw Katie's jaw drop.

'He is the fifth richest man in Britain you know,' Sandra explained. 'He inherited his wealth from his parents but he has always kept an interest in his newspapers.'

'He hardly needs to work, does he?' the student commented, gazing round at the grandeur that now surrounded her.

'No, but like all of us he needs a reason to get up in the morning,' the older woman replied, as they walked up the steps to the front door. A well-dressed young man greeted them at the top.

'I'm Gregory, Mr Duff's assistant,' the man, in his early twenties said, introducing himself. 'Mr Duff is waiting for you in the drawing room.'

'Thank you Gregory,' Sandra said, with the confidence of someone who had visited the stately home on several occasions.

'Sandra, how lovely to see you! So glad you could come tonight,' said Mr Duff as he greeted his editor with the utmost charm. 'And this must be our reporter of the year!'

'Mr Duff, may I introduce Katie Baxter,' Sandra said politely.

The tall, fit looking, gentleman, in his early seventies, reached across and firmly shook Katie's hand.

'Well done young lady. Sandra told me this was all your own work; the article was extremely well put together. Would you ladies like a sherry?' Mr Duff asked.

'Not for me thank you, I'm driving,' Sandra reminded her boss. 'A soft drink would be good though.'

'Yes, please,' the young student piped up.

'Gregory, see to that please. I'll have my usual,' the older man instructed.

'Now Katie,' he continued. 'I hear from Sandra, that you're a very interesting young lady, as well as talented. Something about you and your brother surviving an air crash and months of living among the tribespeople of the Amazon jungle. Tell me about it, sounds remarkable.'

Gregory returned with the refreshments as Katie launched into her story. She found it quite difficult at times but managed to tell her tale. Mr Duff was astute enough to pick up that there was something troubling her.

'Where is your brother now?' he enquired.

After so many sleepless nights worrying about her brother, the question was too much for Katie and she burst into tears. Sandra was shocked and didn't know how to react but Mr Duff, despite his pompous appearance and behaviour, was quick to comfort the student. He knelt beside the young lady gently encouraging her to unburden herself. Within a few minutes Katie had blurted out the story of Tim's kidnap and current dangerous mission with the marines.

'It's the not knowing that's the problem, isn't it? I commanded a brigade of marines in the Bosnian war. If the US forces are half as good as our guys, your brother will be absolutely fine. Try not to worry,' he said, encouragingly.

'I have an offer for you Katie, which I hope you'll accept,' Mr Duff declared, cleverly changing the subject.

'Whenever I come across a young person with considerable talent and compassion, I like to help them along a bit. I understand you'll soon be in your final year at university; I would like to offer you a graduate trainee position with my national paper *The London Daily Courier* starting when you finish university,' Mr Duff pronounced.

Katie glimpsed across at Sandra who looked as delighted as Katie felt. The youngster knew how difficult it was to get a job but an offer like this was truly amazing. Katie had heard that national papers often had as many as five hundred applicants for graduate trainee posts and if short-listed, applicants had to go through three days of assessments.

'Yes please!' she replied without a minute's hesitation. The "LDC" was held in high esteem around the globe so this would be an excellent opportunity to get her investigative journalism career off to a flying start.

'That's settled then. The HR department will send you the necessary paper work,' Mr Duff confirmed. 'Here comes the coffee; thank you Gregory.'

'Well done Katie. What a tremendous opportunity for

you; I should know because I was one of LDC's first graduate trainees when the programme started,' Sandra said,
congratulating her student friend.

'And an excellent trainee as well,' Mr Duff commented,
smiling courteously towards Sandra.

'I see you're looking at the portrait above the fireplace,
Katie. Do you recognise him? He was my great, great,
grandfather on my mother's side, William Wilberforce.

'I do know about him; he was the great campaigner who
fought to end the slave trade,' Katie answered, knowledg-
ably. 'He was the subject of several documentaries a few
years ago to mark the two hundred year anniversary of
the Abolition of Slavery Act in 1807, which made slavery
illegal in Britain.'

'That's correct. A couple of things I bet you didn't know
about him. Firstly, that he died three days after the British
parliament passed the 1833 Abolition of Slavery Act,
which abolished slavery in most of the British Empire; it
really was his lifetime's achievement. Secondly, there's a
famous Wilberforce quote: he said "*You may choose to
look the other way, but you can never say again that you
did not know.*"'

Mr Duff had a sip of his whisky before continuing.

'From the amount of work and the quality of the feature
you have produced Katie; you most certainly have not
looked the other way,' he declared.

'Thank you. I'm just so shocked that such awful things
are still going on. If I had known the quote, I would have
included it at the bottom of the article,' Katie said, with a
hint of frustration.

'Don't beat yourself up, Katie. I'm not sure that Graham
at the *Tribune* would have left it in anyway. He doesn't

like to accuse his readership or make them feel guilty; it's not his style,' Sandra commented.

'Ladies, I'm sorry but I have an engagement later tonight so we must say goodbye now. Katie, lovely to meet you and I'm sure our paths will cross again. Sandra, good work at *The Herald*, thank you,' Mr. Duff said, as he shook each by the hand.

'Good night and thank you,' Katie replied.

Sandra dropped Katie off at her flat an hour later. The conversation on the way home had been non stop. Sandra was genuinely excited for Katie.

'Have a good weekend Katie. I hope you get some news of your brother soon,' Sandra said, encouragingly.

'I hope so. Mr. Duff really cheered me up. These marines will be the best. Thanks for the lift,' Katie replied, just before she closed the car door.

By the time Katie arrived home it was too late to pack and head up to London and she was exhausted anyway. Luke phoned to find out if she had heard anything of Tim and how the visit to the boss had gone. It was an hour later when Katie finally hung up her phone; she couldn't believe she had talked to Luke for that long. She knew their friendship was deepening.

Chapter 20

Dawn Raid

Major Irving made the upcoming raid sound all too easy at the briefing. Tim and Miguel could see he was a very experienced soldier, his very persona commanded the admiration of his men. Importantly though not just his men, as the Peruvian army contingent were impressed by the way he handled himself and the way he treated their Captain with such respect.

The plan was to speed-boat up river, as close as they dare, to the Baron's hideout. Then a scout party of the Major, Tim, Miguel and Gigo would paddle ahead and locate the compound and the hut where Rick was held. Major Jack and his commandos would then move into position on the jungle side encircling the mine. At zero five hundred hours, one hour before dawn, they would strike. The commandos would take out as many sentries, silently if possible, as they could. The Major and Tim would locate Rick while the Peruvian marines would carry out an overwhelming frontal assault from the river.

'What could possibly go wrong?' Tim muttered under his breath.

The US advance party left promptly, thirty minutes after

the briefing. Rico and the other warriors would follow with the Peruvian marines. The journey upstream was noisy but cool with much spray thrown up by the rib as it ploughed against the powerful current of the Rio Tigre. When the scout party entered the final tributary Gigo signalled to Major Jack to cut engines. The compound was now about thirty minutes paddling away but he knew there was an abandoned shack up ahead on the far bank where a look-out watched the river. This first-hand knowledge was so important to the success of the mission. The boat was manoeuvred into the bank about a hundred metres from the hut, as by then the men could just make out the outline of the building in the moonlight. Clouds were coming in from the west bringing with them a thunderstorm; great forks of lightning were illuminating the horizon to the left.

Three US commandos left the vessel and swiftly climbed the three metre muddy bank onto the grass above. They had a job to do and Tim knew they wouldn't fail. Ten minutes later all three returned … mission accomplished!

The main force remained two hundred metres behind the scout boat, hugging the high banks on the right. In the dry season the water was so low and the banks so high that they offered excellent shelter in the shadows; it made it very difficult for Tim to see the following boats which, of course, was good. Gigo took the scout boat as far as he dare. He had been before with other warriors and knew a secluded route around the side of the compound. Eight men plus Tim, Miguel and Gigo scrambled up the bank and into the jungle. Very quickly Gigo found the narrow path he was looking for; he led the way with the commandos hot on his heels but suddenly he stopped, rooted to the spot. He had heard movement up ahead; the jungle birds and animals had fallen silent. Someone was coming! A quick signal from the lead commando and everyone disappeared from the track. Two of the Baron's men were patrolling; they were allowed to walk past the first five or six guys and then they were taken down, knocked out cold and without a sound. Two of the marines quickly bound and gagged the men and pushed them into the undergrowth to be picked up at the end of the mission.

So far so good! Tim thought. Another five minutes up the track and the compound came into view through the trees. Through their night sights the commandos saw the guards around the perimeter; Major Jack counted ten in all. But there were also two outside Rick's hut and two on the veranda of the saloon.

'To do this properly we need another eight guys up here, Sarge. Get them sent up from the second boat, pronto. I think this storm is going to hit just at the right time. Their fighters are going to be watching the pyrotechnics and not concentrating on the job in hand so we should get the upper hand. Thirty minutes until the off. As soon as the others arrive we'll move everyone into position,' Major Jack Irving instructed with his usual nonchalance.

The reinforcements arrived within fifteen minutes and all were then quickly deployed to their targets. Miguel and Gigo remained at the edge of the clearing but Tim went with the Major and three other GIs to Rick's hut. The Major positioned himself to take the sentry on the left, the young commando the guy on the right. Tim and the other two remained behind the hut. The instructions were that as soon as Rick was free he would go with Tim back to Miguel and Gigo and head towards the waiting boats. As soon as Rick was aboard they had to return to Intuto.

Two minutes until all hell would let loose Tim thought, as he looked at his watch. A huge crack of thunder made him leap so much that the soldier crouching next to him grabbed his arm and smiled. Then the heavens opened; the rain came down in sheets, just what they needed.

'Thank you, God,' Tim whispered.

'Do you believe in God?' the soldier asked.

'Yes, I certainly do,' Tim replied.

'Me too,' came the whispered reply.

The Major and his co-partner simultaneously pounced, neutralising the guards. The door of the hut was unlocked and quickly everyone was inside. Then the firing started. Tim was too busy searching for Rick to see what was going on outside. Eventually he made out the frame of a man huddled on a mat in the corner.

'Rick, are you alright? It's Tim, we've come to get you out of here,' Tim shouted above the noise of battle.

Tim shook his friend expecting him to waken and greet them, but the doctor couldn't rouse him. Tim searched for Rick's pulse; it was rapid and feeble. The young medic tried to waken his patient again but he could only raise a groan. Tim could feel Rick was hot with fever and the smell around him told Tim he had been vomiting.

'Major, Rick is sick. Possibly malaria, maybe dysentery. He is very dehydrated we need to get him back to Intuto for fluids and full assessment as quickly as possible,' Tim said anxiously, as he continued to examine Rick as best he could.

'Just as soon as we neutralise the bad guys,' the Major replied. 'Our medic, Corporal Brown, carries fluids for intravenous replacement. Once things quieten down a little I'll get him over here.'

The noise was terrific. Tim found it really hard to concentrate and he needed to because he had a very sick guy on his hands. Several minutes later, to find out how things were progressing, he peered through the slats in the wall. He could see that the saloon was on fire; the girls were streaming out of the building and heading for the jungle. It looked as if there were many casualties lying around the village, hopefully only terrorists, he thought. The Peruvian commandos were still pouring over banks from the river below but they were now in every area of the compound. Soon the only firing was coming from the Baron's house.

Suddenly a loudhailer boomed over the compound. The Peruvian Captain told his men to cease fire and called on the Baron to surrender. At first nothing happened so Captain Garcia repeated his call to surrender.

Slowly the door of the Baron's house opened and out came Raquel carrying her new baby, followed by Carolina and two other women who Tim didn't know. To everyone's surprise the Baron followed, waving a white flag; his fighters then quickly laid down their arms as they knew the odds were stacked against them.

'I didn't think he would give up that easy,' Major Jack said as he watched the events unfold. 'I'd heard he was a real tough nut.'

The Major was quickly on the radio advising his men to watch out for an ambush, this all seemed too easy he thought. By dawn the marines had checked every hut and every part of the mine. The remaining fighters were disarmed, bound and huddled into one area and watched over by heavily armed Peruvian marines. The Baron was held separately in his house and was interrogated briefly by both Major Irving and the Peruvian Captain.

Gigo and Miguel had come to the village to find out what was happening. When they realised the young girls had taken off into the jungle they went after them. Fortunately Gigo shouted his sisters' names and they responded; in total thirty-two girls retuned to the compound. The marines discovered a stockade area close to the mine workings where they found fifty-seven young men and boys crushed into a small unsanitary makeshift building.

Once the sun was up Tim was able to get a better look at Rick. He was very dehydrated and had a high fever. Fortunately the US medic, Corporal Clint Brown, arrived to help Tim and between them they put an intravenous line into Rick's arm and quickly started him on fluids. Rico arrived and checked over the patient as well, his knowledge of tropical illnesses was invaluable to Tim.

'When we get him back to Intuto, I can test his blood for malaria. If that's the diagnosis I have the correct treatment in the clinic,' the young nurse offered, 'but it might not be malaria.'

'That's great! We need to get him to the clinic as soon as possible,' Tim replied, wondering how long until it would be safe to move Rick.

The unit medic left to check on the rest of the men. Two of the guys had minor wounds but mercifully there had been no fatalities. Three terrorists had been killed and eleven wounded. The Peruvian medics were patching them up. Another thirty-five terrorists were now in captivity and it was hoped that none had escaped into the jungle.

Major Irving and Captain Garcia left the Baron's house and were making their way across to see how Tim was getting on with Rick. Suddenly shots rang out. Tim looked outside and saw Major Irving fall to the ground.

'Sniper!' roared Garcia from the ground where he had dived beside the Major. 'Medic! We need the medic now! The Major's been hit.'

A barrage of small arms fire was shot into the jungle in the direction of the sniper, long enough for the Major to be dragged by his men to the cover of Rick's hut. Tim slipped out to assess the wounded man; Corporal Brown joined him from across the compound.

Quickly Tim applied pressure to the main leg artery to stop the bleeding and the army medic swiftly placed a bandage over the wound. Next, Tim inserted an intravenous needle to give the Major fluids to compensate for his blood loss. The officer was in excruciating pain from his shattered thigh bone so before moving him into the hut beside Rick he was given a shot of morphine.

US Marine Lieutenant Buddy Clark arrived ten minutes later to report that the sniper had been neutralised and that the Peruvian marines were securing a half kilometre cordon round the compound. As soon as that was done the US contingent would leave for Intuto with Major Jack, Rick and Tim.

'How are you, Sir?' the lieutenant asked.

'It could have been worse,' he said with a slightly euphoric smile from his morphine. 'It's your show now Buddy.'

'We'll get you home real soon Jack,' the young officer promised. 'Just as soon as the Peruvians have the perimeter properly secured we'll head back to Intuto.'

'Can we take Rico with us?' Tim asked. 'He has the skills to identify the type of malaria Rick may have, so we can start treatment as soon as we are back in Intuto.'

'Sure, no problem. Be ready to move out in twenty minutes,' the lieutenant said as he left to check on his men.

Tim and Corporal Brown spent the time checking that the patients were in the best shape they could be prior to being moved to the navy boats; the bouncing about on the river would be difficult for them. The army medic splinted the Major's leg to make him as comfortable as possible. But another burst of gunfire from the jungle made them realise that it might be more that twenty minutes before it was safe to make a dash for the boats.

Chapter 21

Decisions

Rick had coped with the journey back to Intuto better than anyone could have hoped. His conscious level had improved, his pulse was much stronger and his heart rate had come down. Tim was pleased that the fluids they had pumped into him were beginning to correct his patient's dehydration. However, the blood test Rico had carried out on Rick showed that there was no evidence of malaria. Not having a proper diagnosis was troubling Tim greatly; he began to realise his limited knowledge of tropical diseases was beginning to show, but at least his patient was stable for now.

Rico stripped off Rick's few clothes so Tim could examine him properly and in a decent amount of daylight. The nurse noted areas of tiny bruises on Rick's skin.

'I think Rick probably has dengue. Come and look at his skin Tim,' the young nurse said.

'You've seen dengue before Rico? I haven't,' said Tim. 'Are you sure this is dengue?

'Yes, I've seen it many times; it's a very common disease in the tropics and I think this is likely to be the serious form of dengue.'

'Then we don't have much time, we need to get him to a main hospital and fast,' Tim said.

Just at that moment Lieutenant Buddy walked in to see how the patients were doing. Tim explained that the Major was stable and comfortable but that he was greatly concerned about Rick.

'The medevac chopper is on its way from our base in Columbia. It should be here within the hour. When he realised Rick was seriously unwell the Major contacted HQ and requested evacuation as soon as possible. It'll work out well for him too. Both will be in a state of the art hospital by midnight tonight, I promise you.'

'Oh that's a relief. I wouldn't have fancied Rick's chances if he stayed here.'

'Neither would I,' the lieutenant commented as he looked round the clinic. 'But you've done a great job Doc, looking after these guys as well as you have. There'll be two military surgeons on board with all the best gear so you'll get the assistance you need shortly. How's the Major doing?'

'He's still sleeping. I think the boat trip took a lot out of him, despite the morphine. I gave him some more ten minutes ago; it seems to have done the trick,' Tim informed the officer.

'Good. There's a heavy guard around the clinic and throughout the town. We don't want any 'Black Vulture' sympathisers having a go at us again. After the chopper has been we'll hang around until the Peruvian marines show and then we'll return to base. What about you Tim? Once the word is out that the Baron has been captured some of the group's followers might come after you. I don't want to worry you, but these guys can be real vengeful. And you, gringo Doc, stick out like a sore thumb!' Buddy explained, with a smile.

'He's right Tim, you have to think about leaving the Amazon,' Rico chipped in. 'You've done so much for my people but you've to look out for yourself now. I bet when Miguel gets back he'll say the same.'

'I hadn't really thought about it like that but I suppose you're right,' Tim replied, as he began to consider his predicament.

The Major stirred and called Buddy over; he had overheard the conversation about Tim.

'Get that boy on the chopper with me,' he whispered. 'These "Vultures" will come after him, there's no doubt. Make sure the people of Intuto see him board the chopper, so no one gets hurt in the town either.'

'I'll do my best to persuade him, Sir, but I'm not sure,' Buddy remarked, doubtfully.

'Did you hear that, Tim?' Buddy asked the young doctor.

'Yes, but I still have work to do in Nueva Casa,' Tim answered, despondently.

'The best thing you can do for the villagers of Nueva Casa is to leave,' Rico advised. 'You put them at serious risk if you stay there.'

'I suppose you're right. I would be heading back to Lima in another two weeks anyway. I don't want to put anyone in jeopardy either. So I guess it's time to go,' Tim conceded, reluctantly.

'Good decision. I'll radio HQ and let them know,' Buddy said as he marched out of the clinic.

'I won't even have a chance to say goodbye to Miguel', Tim moaned, as he slumped into a chair.

'Hey my friend, you've done a tremendous job here. If it wasn't for you, Rick wouldn't have been rescued or the Baron captured,' Rico reminded his friend.

'And what about you, Rico?' Tim asked. 'Will you be safe here?'

'I'm not afraid. They know I was there but I was just doing my job. I didn't lead the army to the camp. Besides, God will take care of me; He has a plan for my life and I intend to follow it. He must have some special work for me to do. Why else did He rescue me from the streets?' Rico said, with a big grin of gratitude.

'You're already doing a great job here. You're good at your work and you're really skilled in the operation room. When's the new doctor due to arrive?' Tim asked.

'Next month,' Rico replied. 'I've worked with him in Libertad; he's a good doctor too.'

'Right let's do it. Let's get these men as good as we can before the transport arrives,' Tim said jumping out of his chair. Once he had made his mind up Tim moved fast; it was indecision he couldn't cope with, his or anybody else's.

The two men attended to their patients making sure they were as stable and comfortable as possible. Tim checked through his rucksack, the marines had recovered it from the compound. At first he thought things had been removed but after a couple of minutes he found what he was looking for ... his passport. Phew! that could have been tricky he thought to himself.

'Rico, I'm so glad that we've met up again. After Katie and I were rescued in Iquitos all those years ago, each time we met Gilberto, the first thing we would ask him was "have you found Rico?" You see, you saved our lives; without you the police would have left us to their dogs. If you and Andres hadn't pulled us into that building and then taken us to your hideout in the sewer, we wouldn't be having this conversation; Katie and I would've been killed,' Tim spoke, full of emotion.

Rico reached out to steady his friend, 'Hey amigo, it's OK. You would have done it for me. On the streets we learnt to look out for one another.'

'Thanks Rico. But what's so distressing about that horrible time was that the policemen believed that by getting rid of a couple of street kids they would be cleaning up the neighbourhood, doing their civic duty. How awful is that?'

'Street kids are treated like rats because they have to live like rats: hated by people, living in sewers, raking through rubbish bins for scraps of food, beaten or killed and then thrown on the tip. That's the way it is,' Rico lamented, now psychologically back on the streets.

'We so wanted to rescue you from the streets, Rico, do something to help you. Eventually we presumed you had been killed or died a horrible death, just like Andres, beaten by security guards! I know Katie will be ecstatic when she hears you've survived and are doing extremely well,' Tim said, as he reached out to embrace his friend.

'I used to wonder if you'd met up with your parents and returned to Lima. Gilberto was such a good man, I knew he would look after you,'

'Mum and Dad flew into Iquitos first thing the next day. It was a wonderful reunion. Have you met up with your mother, Rico?' Tim asked sensitively.

'No, I've looked for her in Belen, but I was told she had died of fever.'

'I'm sorry, Rico.'

'Hey! It's been an honour for me to meet you again, Tim, and to have worked with you here in the jungle,' Rico said, lightening the mood of the conversation. 'God blesses those who have suffered injustice as we've seen today: the freeing of Rick and all those young slaves. The Baron and his men will be thrown into prison for a very long time. Now that's justice after all they have done!'

'Yeah, you're right!' Tim replied.

'So it is with me, I have a good life now; I'm a respected member of Peruvian society, I'm no longer a street kid, hated and abused by everyone. I can vote, I've a girl and we plan to get married next year in Iquitos. We'll have kids and they'll go to school,' Rico declared with a huge grin.

'Rico, that's terrific news! Congratulations. What's her name? Have you a photograph?' Tim asked, excitedly.

'Yes. I've a picture here in my locket,' Rico said, as he pulled the chain from under his shirt. 'Her name is Maribel. Would you and Katie do us the honour of coming to our wedding?'

'Rico, we would love to. I know Katie will be thrilled. She often speaks about you. Maribel looks really "cool". What does she do?' Tim enquired of his friend.

'She's a teacher in Iquitos. I miss her very much; I'll not see her for another five months,' Rico groaned.

'Gilberto would love to meet you again too. He's easy to find. I'll give you his cell phone number. When I'm home, I'll contact him and let him know we met up. He'll be delighted; he's such a wonderful guy. He's out late into the night four nights a week feeding street boys.

'That would be so cool. I'd love to thank him for all he does for the kids on the street.'

'Hey, speaking of cell phones, I've just remembered I can take your photograph, Rico. Let's hope it's where I left it, in the side pocket of my rucksack, and that there's some battery left,' Tim said, as he rushed over to search his belongings again.

Tim was delighted; his phone was still there and working. He took several photographs of Rico to take home to show to his family and email to Gilberto.

The sound of the approaching chopper finished the photo shoot. Soon four US army medical personnel swooped into the clinic. The surgeon lieutenant introduced himself to Tim who quickly gave him a history of each patient and their current 'stats'. The marine medics assessed each casualty and much to Tim's professional satisfaction decided that nothing else needed to be done before the evacuation, each man was stable.

Tim was never good at farewells but confirmed he would make sure he was free to come to Rico's wedding next August. The two friends embraced before Tim ran for the helicopter watched by a large crowd of Intuto inhabitants. Within ten minutes of landing the chopper was airborne again with the casualties and Tim on board.

The chopper swooped low over the Rio Tigre before sweeping north east towards the Columbian border. Tim peered down over the myriad of snaking rivers that made up this region of Amazonia. The young doctor watched for the Peruvian army returning to Intuto with their captives. He had hoped to catch a glimpse of the flotilla coming down the Tigre, but he couldn't see any sign of them or the mine either and yet Tim was sure they would be flying over the area.

He was more relaxed now; his patients were now in the care of highly trained emergency medics working with the most sophisticated equipment money could buy. How he wished he could have stayed longer and at least look after

Nueva Casa until the new doctor arrived but he knew it was right that he was on his way home. Or was he? What was he going to do? It suddenly occurred to him that he was leaving the jungle for a completely different country. Was he going to fly from Columbia to Lima and back to Iquitos or was he heading back to London?

Chapter 22

Commando Base

The marine base was just over the border into Columbia. A heavily fortified military community with evidence of both army and air force units. The patients were immediately dispatched to the military hospital and Tim escorted to the officers' mess where he met Sergeant Tyler Smith of the US army.

'Dr Baxter, I'm instructed to billet you in the officers' mess and to make sure you're looked after here on the base. I understand that you've been on a very arduous expedition and that you may need some time to recover. You're welcome to stay until you feel ready to travel to Bogotá airport for your flight,' the Sergeant explained to Tim as he ushered him along the corridor to a very clean and air-conditioned room. 'As soon as you know your destination please let me know and I'll organise your flight.'

'Thanks'

'Showers are two doors along, Sir; I'll bring you some clean clothes. Colonel Menzies would like to debrief you at eighteen hundred hours,' the Sergeant continued.

'Any chance of some food, Sarge? I'm starved,' Tim asked, catching a whiff of some freshly brewed coffee from the mess lounge.

'Sure thing. If you go and clean up, I'll be back in about half an hour with the clothes then I'll take you to the canteen. Unfortunately you have to be escorted around the base, but I'm sure you understand,' the Sergeant said as he left.

Tim flung himself on the bed and just lay there thinking over the last few days. What a rollercoaster, he thought.

Sergeant Smith was gently shaking him when he came to.

'What time is it?' Tim asked.

'It's sixteen hundred hours. You've been out cold for the last two hours but I need to get you tidied up before I take you to see the Colonel, so time to rise and shine,' the big Sergeant said with a smile.

'Thanks for letting me sleep. I don't know when I last slept. Where's the shower?'

At eighteen hundred hours Tim was washed, shaved, smartly dressed and he had eaten a proper meal; he was ready to meet the Colonel. The Colonel's office was across the base. Tim passed US soldiers and Columbian men on the way. He could see this was a busy camp attached to a Columbian Air Force base. There were several attack helicopters around the perimeter of the landing strip with a couple of small spotter planes sitting away to his left.

Just as he was about to mount the steps to the command building he noticed in a hangar about fifty metres away, two drone spy planes. Tim had heard about these on the news channels; they were the US Air Force's very efficient, unmanned, surveillance aircraft, but sometimes they carried bombs, as they had in Afghanistan, with devastating effect.

Colonel Doug Menzies was a tall, ginger-haired man, in his early forties, Tim thought. He made the young doctor very welcome.

'Dr Baxter, I have been instructed by the US Government to thank you for your help in the freeing of the hostage Rick Jefferson. The Black Vultures terrorist group has evaded us for several months; your information was the vital lead we needed. Our sources had pointed to a gold mine in the south of Peru as the prime location for Rick but we could never prove it, now we know why,' the Colonel said.

'Do you know how Rick is doing? Would I be able to go and see him and speak with the medics?' Tim asked, afraid the hospital might be off limits to him, a civilian.

'Sure once we're finished here, Sergeant Smith will take you over,' Colonel Menzies replied.

'Do you know if the Peruvian marines managed to free all the young women who were held in the terrorist camp?' Tim enquired of the officer. 'It was disgusting to see; many of these women were no more than girls.'

'We've had no formal reports as yet, but I do know from previous raids where we have worked with this Peruvian unit that they are first class. Recently the Peruvian government has put in a great deal of effort into stopping the trafficking of young Peruvian women into remote locations in the jungle, usually by illegal mining companies. So I'd imagine they would be even less tolerant of terrorists like the Baron,' the Colonel replied, encouragingly.

'That's good to hear but it wasn't just young girls who had been trafficked into that site; there must have been many boys working in dreadful conditions in the mine,' Tim explained.

'It's usually the poor who fall victim to traffickers, as we've seen in this case; I'll bet many of the workforce have been kidnapped from the tribespeople in the south of Peru. They're then transported up river well away from their own backyard, so to speak, that way they daren't try to escape because they don't know how to get home. We've seen this scenario in other terrorist camps; only last year we busted a cocaine production operation deep in the jungle here in Columbia. The boss had sent his men a hundred miles down the Rio Napo and raided villages to abduct the young girls and teenage boys. They were used as slaves and suffered all sorts of terrible cruelties so none ever tried to escape,' the Colonel further expounded.

'The Baron's mistake must've been to allow his men to kidnap local girls; I wouldn't have been able to lead your men back to the mine if it hadn't been for Gigo and his friends. They knew exactly where the camp was because their sisters had been taken there; they were so angry they couldn't rescue them but they knew they had no chance against heavily armed men,' Tim related to the Colonel.

'Good point. Once the Baron has worked out the mistake that led to his capture, the man who made the error will have to watch his back; this guy is renowned for his cruelty and his organisation has a long reach,' the Colonel commented. 'Which brings me to you; I've managed to have a short debrief with Major Irving. He feels strongly that your life could still be in danger, his advice is that at least for now you get out of, not just Peru, but South America.'

'I was hoping to go back to Lima for a few days and meet up with some friends there,' Tim complained bitterly.

'Tim I don't think you realise just how big a fish we've caught,' the Colonel cautioned. 'This man is the co-founder of the Vultures with his brother Gustav. Gustav's reputation is even worse than the Baron's and he has a huge price on his head; he is still very much at large somewhere in

South America. My advice to you, Tim, is that as soon as you are ready, you fly out back to the UK.'

'It's that serious, wow! Oh well, that rules out Lima. Thank you, Colonel Menzies for your frankness; I would think I'll be on my way sometime tomorrow if the Sergeant can get me booked on a flight,' Tim accepted, now realising there really wasn't any alternative but to leave South America.

'Back to London?' the Colonel checked.

'Not sure yet. I'm due to start a locum job in Sydney, Australia, in a month's time but after all that's happened in the last week or so, I do quite like the thought of going home to London for a while,' Tim said, considering his options.

'Sleep on it Tim, just let the Sergeant know in the morning. Good to meet you and all the best for your future career,' the Colonel said shaking Tim's hand.

'Thank you,' Tim said, as he left to go to the hospital to see Rick and Major Jack.

Tim was escorted across to the military hospital where he was introduced to Lieutenant Colonel Kurt Grieg the commanding officer of the hospital.

'You did a fine job with Rick. If you hadn't been on hand to give him that initial treatment he wouldn't have made it. Well done Doc,' the army medic said to Tim shaking his hand profusely.

'Did you know he had dengue? He must have had it before because he has had the severe form. But he is conscious now and stable so you can go and speak with him if you like. Major Irving is in the next bay. His leg is in a mess so we're taking him for surgery in about an hour's time; we'll need to plate his thigh bone. Give him three months and he'll be up and at it, but not in any combat role. He's due to leave the army next year anyway; fortunately his wound is not going to hold him back in civilian life,' the medic continued.

'I've never seen dengue; I've only read about it in text books. Your army medic helped rehydrate him. You have a highly trained bunch of guys working in your marine units,' Tim replied, slightly embarrassed by the officer's praise.

'Only the best, Tim! Only the best. Come I'll take you to Rick,' the medic said as he ushered Tim along the corridor.

Rick certainly looked better than he had the last time Tim had seen him, but he was still very weak. When he saw Tim coming he managed a smile to greet his young friend. The Colonel left the two men in peace to talk.

'I'm so glad to see you Tim. No one here knew anything about you, if you were alive or dead. How are you?' Rick asked, in a very soft, hesitant voice as he reached out to Tim.

Tim realised very quickly that Rick could remember nothing of his rescue, so the young doctor pulled up a chair beside the bed and told the former hostage everything from the capsize of the canoe, to the assault on the compound, right through to their chopper evacuation to the army base.

'I owe you my life on two counts, Tim. When we arrived back at the mine the Baron was furious. The young Colombian guy who was steering our boat, when it hit the submerged tree trunk catapulting us all into the river, was tied overnight to a post in the middle of the compound. In the morning the Baron came out of his hut, walked straight across to him and shot him in the head with his pistol. I know – I watched him do it through the slats in my prison.

That man is absolutely ruthless, the lad could only have been in his early twenties, about the same age as my boy,' Rick said, with tears welling up in his eyes.

'Don't worry Rick; the Baron is going to be locked away for a very long time,' Tim said trying to console his friend.

'The next day the Baron left by fast boat to Ecuador but sent his henchman across to see me first. He informed me that the US government had replied to their ransom demands; they were refusing to pay! He told me to say my prayers because they were going to execute me when the Baron returned. I asked how long did I have and he said two days! Later that day I became sick with a very high fever and that's all I remember,' Rick explained, pulling at the bed clothes in his distress.

'Well the Baron was at home when we came calling with the Peruvian marines, so I guess he must have changed his mind about shooting you Rick,' Tim said, trying to lighten the mood.

'No, he was not an early riser. I bet he came back to the mine the night before you attacked and that I was one of his late morning chores. He always did the executions himself ... such a sadist; he loved to have the power over life and death,' Rick corrected.

'Did you see him kill many people in the time you were held captive?' Tim asked.

'Anyone who crossed him; he loved to make an example of them ... bang! If any of the labour force tried to escape, or were caught with any gold on them at the end of the day... bang! A ruthless, ruthless man,' Rick concluded, wildly looking from right to left as he relived in his mind the awful things he had witnessed.

'It's OK Rick; it's all behind you now. Time you rested.

I'll come back and see you tomorrow before I leave,' Tim assured his friend.

'Are you going home? When will I see you again? You must come and visit me in the States. Come for a holiday; meet my darling wife and our family. Tim, I owe you so much,' Rick said, becoming quite emotional.

'Rick you concentrate on getting better; and yes, I would love to come to the States to visit, but you must get strong first and enjoy time with your family,' Tim said trying to calm his friend. 'After talking with you I've made up my mind. My folks are home on leave from India; for the next month they will be in London so I'm going to join them and my sister Katie. You are right; families are so important, travelling round the world can wait! Cheers Rick, see you before I leave tomorrow,' Tim said as he left to pay a quick visit to the Major.

The nurse had just finished giving Major Irving his pre-med as Tim put his head round the curtain.

'Hi Tim, good to see you lad,' the Major said, in a slightly euphoric manner that reminded the young doctor that morphine certainly keeps the patient happy.

'Good to see you too, Major. I hear that very shortly, they're going to give you a bionic thigh bone,' Tim teased.

'Steady on there. Last I heard it was a metal plate; anything that gets me out of this blasted bed is fine by me! I hate being a patient,' the officer bleated.

'It'll certainly hasten your recovery; you'll be off home on leave in no time,' Tim reassured him.

'How's Rick doing? Nobody tells me anything in here,' the Major asked, concerned for the other sick man.

'He's much better than when we found him that's for sure. By all accounts we got him out of there in the nick of time; he says the Baron was going to execute him because the US government wouldn't pay the ransom. So a great job Major Jack, you and your marines,' Tim replied. 'And thanks for making sure I came out on the helicopter. I've learned a lot about the Baron and how ruthless he was. Your Colonel Menzies didn't mince his words either when I was debriefed.'

'We've been after the Baron for a while now and we've seen a lot of his dirty tricks. I hope you've been persuaded to leave South America, Tim?'

'Yes, I've decided to head home to London for a few weeks, and then probably take up my post in Australia in October. Do you know when you'll be flown back to the States?' Tim asked hoping the officer would be back among his family soon.

'I guess it depends how quickly I recover from this op. But there's a first rate military Rehab Centre in Miami, not far from my home town so I'm hoping I'll end up there. I can't wait to see my wife and kids again. We've a little one of five months and a daughter of five years, so I'm really blessed,' the Major replied, suddenly feeling home sick.

'The baby, is it a boy or a girl?'

'She's called Alice. You know I've hardly seen her. That's all going to change though as I'm due to leave the army next June, but maybe with this injury I'll get a medical discharge and be home a bit earlier. I've enjoyed my army life and we have stopped a lot of bad characters, but hey, it's time for me to hand over to the younger guys,' the Major said in reflective mood.

'I'll leave you now, I hear the orderlies coming to take you to the operating room. I'll look back tomorrow before I catch my flight,' Tim said, taking his leave.

'Thanks Tim. I hope you know that we wouldn't have had a successful rescue mission without you. Your brilliant idea to link through to the American Embassy via your father was a life saver, actually many lives. Peru and Columbia will be a much safer place without our friend the Baron,' Major Jack affirmed. 'See you tomorrow.'

Chapter 23

Touchdown

The jumbo jet touched down at Heathrow airport on Sunday morning; it was cold and wet. Tim was met at the airport by his parents in a very emotional reunion. Sarah was her usual tearful self, almost refusing to release her precious son from her grasp.

'Steady on Mum, I'm fine! Nothing happened to me, no one hurt me,' Tim said trying to reassure his mother.

'When I heard you had been kidnapped, I just couldn't believe it. There have been so many terrible things happen to people who have been taken like that,' Sarah said, trying to explain her anxiety. 'It was just like the time we heard your plane had crashed in the Amazon all those years ago.'

'But Mum, you knew I was free by the time you received my message. What were you worrying about?' Tim asked, with the exasperation of a young man.

'Oh just the small matter that you were going back to the terrorist hideout with US marines, to free a hostage and the small matter of not knowing if you were alive or dead for three days. That's what was worrying me. Boys!' Sarah blurted out.

'Oh Mum, you shouldn't get so worried about me. You

know I'm well looked after,' Tim said, as he grabbed his mother for another hug.

'I know! I should have more faith. That's what your Dad said but it wasn't easy especially when we were waiting to hear from you. But here you are, safely home. Come on let's get back to the house and you can tell us all about it,' Sarah explained, wiping her tears away and regaining her composure.

'Dad, are you alright?' Tim asked his father.

'Of course, I'm a man,' he answered, with a glint in his eye. 'Glad to have you home son.'

'Where's Katie? I thought she would be here to meet me, her favourite brother,' Tim asked, as he looked around the arrivals hall.

'Only brother! She knows you're safe but she doesn't know you are coming home today. Katie has been a very busy and successful girl these last few weeks. Wait until you hear her news,' Sarah teased, knowing Tim would be desperate to learn what his little sister had been up to.

'She's getting married! What's his name?' Tim was quick to ask.

'Don't be stupid! She doesn't even have a boyfriend,' Alex replied swiftly, in a father's protective tones.

'Katie has been published in a Sunday magazine! Last weekend,' Sarah said excitedly.

'Really, you're kidding; my little sister!' Tim said in disbelief. 'What was she writing about?'

The trip home took over an hour as the traffic was particularly bad that lunchtime, but no one noticed as the car was full of chatter and laughter; parents reunited with their beloved son. Over lunch Tim related his adventures to his mother and father.

Around three in the afternoon the door bell rang as expected; Tim was ushered to answer the door to his unsuspecting sister.

'Tim, it's you! You're home,' Katie screamed, as she grabbed her brother in a huge hug. 'Why did nobody tell me you were coming home? Mum, Dad you are rascals!'

Alex and Sarah watched from the hall as their two children were reunited. Ever since the two youngsters had survived their terrible ordeal in the jungle they had been very close; always looking out for one another.

The rest of the weekend was spent exchanging news. Sarah and Alex had stories of their work in India too. Alex was pleased with the four schools he had helped to set up in one of the slum areas of Kolkata. Each school had a feeding programme and health provision for Dalit children, India's untouchable class. Sarah told how she had helped expose a sweatshop that was supplying one of Europe's High Street Chains.

Katie recounted how her meeting with Laura had changed her life and made her even more determined to become an investigative journalist, working in the field of human rights. Her job offer from Mr Duff to join his graduate trainee programme was the icing on the cake of a very special summer. Her frustrations about not being free to join Tim in the Amazon over the summer months had all gone. Katie also acknowledged, after her mother's prompting, that she had helped put Laura's story into the public domain and in so doing hopefully made other young girls aware of the dangers out there. Sarah also pointed out that the publication was part of Laura's healing process. Katie wondered where Laura was living and if she would ever hear from her again.

Now that he was safely back home, among his family, Tim began to realise how close he had come to being killed by the terrorists. Once he had successfully delivered Raquel's baby he really had been vulnerable to any whim of the Baron. What if the baby had died? Or if he had mucked up the operation to deliver the infant, or Raquel had died? Tim found himself coming out in a cold sweat as he thought through these various scenarios.

Other things deeply troubled Tim too. He had had no idea about the abduction of young people in South America; put to work as virtual slaves in mines or in the brothels of the shanty towns. He possibly could have understood it since the Baron was part of a terrorist group but the Colonel at the base told him of illegal miners doing the same. Tim supposed it was again the criminal underworld abusing the most vulnerable in their societies, the poor.

Tim was shocked by Katie's article; he had no knowledge that such exploitation was going on in Britain. The information his sister had shared with him about trafficking and modern-day slavery, made him understand that what he had seen for himself in South America was going on all over the world.

As Tim tried to sleep that night he had doubts about his up-and-coming year abroad. He planned to honour the locum he had arranged in Australia but he was uncertain as to what to do next. Perhaps he should apply to do a tropical medicine course because one thing that was clear to him now, was that he was going to dedicate his life to working in the developing world, to try to make a difference ... and most of that world was in the tropics.

Epilogue

Katie returned to university for her final year. The first term was full-on, with little time for anything but her honours assignments. She had to choose a topic for her thesis from a designated list: "Tabloid Sensationalism", "Sports Overkill", "The Newspaper is Dead?", or "Journalism – a Profession at Risk". Katie elected to work on the final option and she was delighted that her tutor accepted her draft proposal which had the working title of "Investigative Journalism Can Change the World?" She knew this work would give her the background she would need to launch her chosen career.

The student spent hours in the library researching successes and failures of historical and contemporary journalists. She read of journalist's feature articles that had launched huge charitable outpourings by the nation, and of articles that brought down governments. Katie began to realise that she could make a difference and improve the world, for at least some people.

The young journalist had experienced great encouragement from the article about Laura. Things had happened as a result of the feature: concerned parents and girls had come forward and reported other cases of grooming, the authorities had examined their procedures and began training their frontline staff on the issues of trafficking and grooming of young people, educators had developed material to take into schools and through drama, videos and workshops were now warning students of the dangers that lay outside. Katie felt really good about these developments but she knew it was as much about Laura's courage as it was about her journalistic skills.

At Christmas time, Katie unexpectedly received an email from Laura. She was settling into her new country and had made new friends. Her first set of exams had gone really well and she was hoping to go to college the following year to study physiotherapy. Laura thanked Katie again for believing her story and helping her get her life back; physiotherapy was something she had always wanted to do and thanks to Katie this was again a possibility.

Tim was accepted for the January intake at the School of Tropical Medicine, which meant he could spend three months in Australia. He planned to fly back to London via the States to visit Rick. The American had been in contact with Tim so the doctor knew that his patient had made a full recovery, nevertheless Rick and his wife had decided that all future employment would be within North America!

It was several weeks before Tim heard from Miguel. Everything in Intuto had quietened down. The army commander had been found guilty at his court martial and was sentenced to ten years in prison. The new commander seemed to be a much fairer man with a better understanding of the indigenous people. Rico was still working in Intuto and was a regular visitor to Nueva Casa; he had become a close friend of Miguel's. Bruno, the chief, died as expected from his failing liver, shortly after Tim had flown out. Miguel planned to stay in Nueva Casa as chief and headmaster but with promised financial help from his brothers in Iquitos, he was going to make sure all his children, daughters and sons went to secondary school.

The Baron was sentenced to life in prison without parole, which in Peru meant he would never walk the streets again. Tim was relieved and delighted when he heard the news. However the advice from Miguel and Gilberto, his friends in Peru, was to stay away from South America for a few years to be absolutely sure the Black Vultures were destroyed. Tim was sad to think that he couldn't visit his friends in Iquitos for a while or attend Rico's wedding but he was a man on a mission and there was no time to lose.

Oh, Katie and Luke continued to see each other. Romance was in the air!

About the Author

Pam Cairns is a Scottish author based in the lovely county of Angus. The author's debut novel 'The Dead Don't Hurt Us' was published in 2010.

'Trampled Shoots' is the second of a series. The first two novels are set in the Amazon jungle of Peru drawing on the author's experiences as a doctor working among the indigenous peoples of the region.

Now retired from medicine, Pam enjoys her new career as a writer. The author is an active member of Soroptimist International, a worldwide organisation which works to improve the lives of women and girls. Pam campaigns to raise awareness of modern-day slavery, an international crime which ensnares millions of men, women, girls and boys around the globe.

Profits from the sale of this book will go to charity.

What is Modern-day Slavery?

When men, women and children are forced to work without pay, under threats of violence to them or their loved ones and when it is impossible for them to walk away … this is slavery.

Modern-day slaves can be found in factories, mines, on cotton farms, fruit farms and construction sites, in restaurants, brothels and private homes. The majority of slaves are under the age of twenty-four years, their young lives brutalised and ruined. Many slaves come from vulnerable poor communities and have been tricked by traffickers with false promises of good jobs or an education. Once they arrive at their destination, which may be across international borders or within their own country, they discover the brutal truth. Poverty often drives parents into the hands of unscrupulous moneylenders; when families can't pay, children are taken into debt bondage. In poor communities parents will often send children to urban households to work in return for food and an education; in reality the children, often as young as five years, enter into a world of domestic servitude where they are denied an education and are at risk of physical and sexual abuse from members of the household. Young boys and girls may be kidnapped, brutalised and forced to be child soldiers; this too is a form of slavery.

Please see our website:
www.trampledshoots.org
for more information

Join us on Facebook
Trampled Shoots

By the Same Author

THE DEAD DON'T HURT US, *so say street children who often hide in the cemeteries of the world,* is a fast-moving, contemporary adventure story based in the hot and dangerous Amazon jungle and the Peruvian city of Iquitos.

A highly stressed, arrogant British oil executive and his wife search for their children who are missing in the rainforest. During the rescue mission, the parents come face to face with the terrible destruction of the rainforest by oil exploration and mining. They come to realise the huge impact this has on the village communities and an ancient way of life.

The children experience the hardships of jungle life, encountering witch doctors and cocaine smugglers along the way. Reaching the jungle city of Iquitos, they are mistaken for street rats. Pursued by the authorities, they hide in the sewers.

An exciting story where love triumphs over evil and hope over despair. A book the author hopes will not only help the reader understand the stresses on the indigenous peoples of the Amazon jungle, but also something of the cruel, loveless life of the street child.

Please visit:
http://www.donthurtus.org
for more information

Available to purchase on:
http://www.amazon.co.uk
both as a paperback and in kindle format.